Stories of
PROFIT
and
LOSS

Bernard Marin

**HARVARD
PUBLICATIONS**

First published in 2019 by
Harvard Publications
432 St Kilda Road
Melbourne 3004

NATIONAL
LIBRARY
OF AUSTRALIA

A catalogue record for this
book is available from the
National Library of Australia

ISBN 9 780648 555308

Design by Skeleton Gamblers Creative

Author's note

The characters and events in these stories are a creation of the author's imagination. They are not intended to portray any person or event, and any likeness they may bear to persons or events past or present is coincidental.

Dedication

For my wife, Wendy; daughters, Amy and Rachel;
daughter-in-law, Deb, and son-in-law Joel; granddaughter,
Goldie, and grandson, Ziggy.

Contents

Office Politics

It was the last week of the financial year. I arrived at work at seven-thirty, parked my car in the basement and stepped into the lift, mentally ticking off my tasks for the day: client meetings, emails, phone calls to canvass what could be done prior to the end of the financial year to minimise tax positions, and there was that inventory of assets and liabilities for probate I needed to prepare for lodgement with the Supreme Court. I stopped on the ground floor to get a short black to jump-start my day – it was going to be busy.

I took the lift to the twenty-sixth floor, found a clear spot on my desk for the espresso, dropped my case in the corner and settled into my chair. There was an hour of peace and silence before the steady waterfall of human noise would interrupt my work, and I intended to make the most of it. Client files and folders almost covered the glass surface of my desk. I sipped my coffee and reached for a file.

At nine I got up from my desk, strode along the corridor and into Troy's office. He was standing at his desk packing photos and other personal items into a box on his side table.

'What are you doing?'

He looked up quickly and swallowed. 'Packing.'

'What? Why?'

'Joanne just told me to leave.'

'What on earth—?' I was stunned. The decision to fire staff was made by *all* the partners. Joanne didn't have the sole authority to hire and fire. 'What on earth is going on?'

'We had an argument; she lost her temper and told me to leave.'

'It's the end of the financial year for god's sake, our busiest time! I need you to prepare an inventory of assets and liabilities today.'

'Tell that to your audit partner,' he said quietly.

'Wait here, don't go anywhere.'

I rushed down the hall to Joanne's office. 'Troy said you've sacked him,' I barked.

'That's right; the less I see of him the better.' Joanne's voice was hard, aggressive.

'What the hell is going on? What's happened?'

Joanne opened her mouth but said nothing. I noticed she couldn't hold my gaze.

'That's not how we do things around here, Joanne. You know you need to get the partners to sign off before you sack somebody.'

'Look, I just don't trust him, Brendan. I've had my doubts for some time. He really slipped up yesterday. It wasn't the first time, and frankly I don't think he should be working here anymore.'

'It's the busiest time of the year, Joanne! We've got clients wanting tax returns lodged, invoices need to go out, creditors have to be paid and we're already short staffed.'

'Bad luck, I want him out,' Joanne said.

I stared at Joanne, noting her jaw clenching as she spoke. I knew there was more to the story. I'd had my eye on Joanne and Troy for some time. 'But he's been a loyal employee – always done his job well. You've never complained about him before. There must be more to it.'

'Look, Brendan, I don't have time to explain now; let's talk later. But be clear: I want him gone.'

I wondered whether my long-held suspicion about their affair was correct. If Troy was telling the truth, and he and Joanne had had an argument, it wasn't fair to sack him. There was more to this than Joanne was admitting. I drew a deep breath. I felt I had no choice but to support my partner's decision – it was a bad look for partners to break ranks in front of staff. I turned and walked back into Troy's office.

'Troy, look, I'm really sorry. Something has obviously happened between the two of you. You have been a good and loyal employee but Joanne seems adamant that you must leave. She's a partner and I have to support her . . .'

He shrugged hopelessly.

'But don't consider this as the termination of your employment. I will investigate further. Maybe it's best if you take some leave now, and once I get some clarity, I'll be in touch.'

For the rest of the day I had trouble concentrating. My mind kept wandering back to Joanne and Troy. I remembered all the times they had come to work at the same time and left five minutes later for breakfast, one through the back door, the other through the front. I recalled seeing them at lunchtime, hunched together in the corner of the local café sipping coffee and murmuring intimately.

That night I stayed back late to catch up on work. Everyone had left – or so I thought – so I was surprised by a knock on my door.

'What are you doing still here?' I said, lifting my head as Joanne opened the door. 'It's late. What's up?'

I noticed Joanne looked a bit dazed: her eyes were red and she seemed lost for words; her face was gaunt and sallow under the fluorescent lights. 'You look terrible,' I said. 'Are you sick? Come in and sit down.'

Joanne took a deep breath, hesitated and said in a faint, uncertain voice, 'I need to tell you something.'

I nodded, indicating a chair.

'I need to tell you the truth about what happened with Troy. I wasn't entirely honest with you before.'

Finally, she's about to fess up, I thought. I had asked Joanne some months ago whether she was having an affair with Troy. Joanne had looked me in the eye and said, *No*. Now she seemed uncomfortable, fidgeting and shifting in her seat and unable to make eye contact.

'Troy and I have been having an affair for the last twelve months,' Joanne said in a rush. 'We had an argument this morning; I lost my temper and told him to leave.'

I looked at Joanne with distaste. I felt anger rise up in me and struggled to contain it. 'As you know, I have long had my suspicions about the two of you. You come to work together, have coffee together, eat lunch together and leave together. But when I asked you if you were having an affair, you vehemently denied it.'

Joanne ran her hand through her curly brown hair, looked at me and said, 'I'm really sorry for lying to you; I'm not proud of it. I wanted to tell you but Troy and I agreed to hide our relationship and wait until we'd separated from our partners and moved in together. I know I've put you in a very difficult position and I'm really sorry for my breach of trust.'

I watched Joanne carefully. Her handkerchief was balled in one hand and there was a frightened look in her eyes.

'Thanks for your apology, Joanne. I can see things have been tricky for you, but we're a week away from the end of the financial year.' I considered my options for a moment and then said, 'I think you should finish up today and take your annual leave.

You need to sort yourself out. I strongly recommend you get some professional help with this.'

'Thanks Brendan, I appreciate it,' Joanne said, dabbing at her forehead and her mouth with the crumpled handkerchief.

I stood and walked her to the door.

On the drive home I went over and over my conversation with Joanne. *Human beings can be so self-destructive*, I thought. I wondered if Joanne's husband, Mark, knew about the affair, and how her three young children would react if their parents separated. Joanne had put herself and the practice in a difficult position. I recalled a recent partners' meeting in which Joanne had urged the partners to increase Troy's salary and I felt fury rise like magma inside me. The deception; the conflict of interest!

Dinner was unusually quiet. Eventually Sarah asked me what was wrong, and I found myself telling my wife about the goings on at work that day and over the last year.

'I'm not surprised,' Sarah said. 'At last year's Christmas party I saw Joanne make a pass at Jane's boyfriend. She's loose, just like her mother.'

'What do you mean?' I cut into my steak.

'Remember the barbecue last July with all the partners and their spouses?'

'Yes.'

'Well, I was talking with Diane. She told me that Joanne's father had left her mother many years ago because she'd had one too many affairs.'

'Go figure. So she's had a good teacher,' I said.

The next morning I woke feeling agitated. I rang Ian, my lawyer, as soon as I got to the office. I needed wise counsel from someone I trusted.

'I've got a problem,' I said as soon as Ian picked up the phone. 'Joanne has been having an affair with Troy – you know Troy, our accountant? The relationship unravelled yesterday and out of the blue, just before the end of the financial year, she sacked him.'

'You'd better come in and see me,' Ian said. 'This is complicated and there's a lot you need to be aware of.'

At eleven-thirty that morning I walked into Ian's office. Sitting opposite him at his large teak desk, I let out a groan of frustrated rage. 'Joanne has been sitting in meetings telling us that Troy needs a pay rise but she never bothered to tell us she was having an affair with him.'

'It's a blatant conflict of interest,' Ian said, shaking his head.

'I know. How can I ever trust her again?'

'You can't,' Ian said flatly. 'Also, an employer has a legal obligation to protect their staff – which you have now breached. You are open to being sued by Troy.'

I felt a coldness move through me. This was worse than I thought. 'What do I do, Ian?'

'Get rid of her,' Ian said. 'I'll have a look at the partnership agreement and get back to you.'

'Wow. That's pretty brutal,' I said. 'She's been with us six years . . .' I stared at Ian, thought for a moment and said, 'I know you're right. Thank you, I appreciate your help.'

I stood up to leave, and felt some of my anxiety dissipate as I felt Ian's warm handshake. I was confident that Ian would help me navigate my way through this minefield.

Sitting at my desk that afternoon I picked up the phone and dialled Troy's number. It rang for some time before he answered it.

'Hello,' he said, his voice cracking.

'How are you feeling?' I asked quietly.

'Annoyed, pissed off – if you really want to know.'

'I understand. I spoke with Joanne and she told me what's been going on.'

'I'm really sorry we've put you in such a difficult position and that I've behaved so badly,' Troy said, his voice sorrowful.

'It's not my place to judge you, Troy,' I said.

'I'm so annoyed with myself. I trusted her because she's supposed to be a decent person. But she manipulated me – made such big promises – and I was stupid enough to believe her.'

'Such as . . .?'

'Oh the usual – we'd set up house, start a new life, you know, all that bullshit. Then she stamped on me like a bug!'

'I'm sorry she treated you that way and if there is anything I can do please tell me. But I want you to know that you are a highly valued employee and we want you back.'

Troy was silent for a long time and I could feel his hesitation.

'She's been stalking me,' he blurted.

'What do you mean?' I said, shocked. I had always suspected Joanne was a good-time girl, but didn't think she would resort to that sort of predatory behaviour.

'It's been going on for a while now, ever since I said I wanted to end it. Driving past my house or ringing me at all hours, parking at the end of the street, watching my every move . . .'

'That is appalling! I'm shocked. I've told her not to come back to the office for a month, but if this continues you may have to take out a restraining order against her.'

The phone went silent and I waited for what seemed a long time.

'Can I take a few more days off please?' Troy asked.

'Of course, take care of yourself and I'll see you when you feel ready to return,' I said as I put down the phone.

I lay in bed listening to the wind in the trees outside the open window. I couldn't sleep. Remembering what my wife had told me about Joanne's mother, I got out of bed and went to my study where I jotted down the names of clients whom I suspected Joanne might have propositioned.

The following morning I arranged to have coffee with one of them, a friend who'd become a client. Jason was a single father, a striking man with a tall, athletic frame and chestnut hair. We met at a restaurant in South Yarra.

'How have you been?' I said.

'Good. Why the sudden call? We haven't spoken in months.'

'I have something in particular to ask you,' I said.

Jason looked at him, his eyes narrowing with suspicion.

I hesitated a moment and said, 'Did you have a relationship with Joanne?'

'Why do you ask?' Jason replied, rotating his glass of sparkling water.

'She's been having an affair with Troy in my office and I wondered who else she had been with.'

Jason looked shocked. He was silent for a moment and then said contemptuously, 'I'm not surprised. We weren't together that long. I took her to a friend's birthday party, found her in the bedroom with her tongue down some guy's throat and said, "We're done!"'

'Thank you for being so honest.'

'It's the least I can do. You've done a lot for me over the years, Brendan.'

'I appreciate it,' I said.

Once back at my desk, I phoned Louis. The phone seemed to ring a long time, but just as I was about to hang up, he answered.

'Hi, it's Brendan. Long time, no speak.'

'I've been busy,' Louis said.

'Do you have a minute?'

'Of course. What's up?'

'I just want to ask you a quick question.'

'If it's about my tax, I'm collecting all my papers and I'll bring them in to you in a week or two.'

'No, actually it's about Joanne.'

There was a long pause. 'What about her?' Louis said carefully.

I hesitated for a few seconds, unsure how to frame the question. 'I'm sorry for prying into your private life, Louis. I know it's not my business, but did you have a relationship with her?'

Louis didn't respond for a moment. Then he said guardedly, 'Why do you ask? We've never discussed anything but work matters.'

'Well, this *is* a work matter. I've got a problem with her and our accountant, Troy, and I think there's a pattern to her behaviour that is putting our firm at risk.'

Louis sighed. 'I'm sorry to hear about all this, Brendan, but I'm not surprised. Our affair was short-lived; she was unfaithful and I finished it within weeks.'

'Are you sure she cheated on you?'

'Absolutely.'

'Thanks, Louis, that's all I need to know.'

The following Monday, I called an extraordinary meeting of partners. I walked into our boardroom and glanced out at the Westgate Bridge on one side and the Dandenong ranges on the other. The view made the room even more impressive. Seated at the large table were Barry and Anthony. I had established the firm with them twenty years earlier and I respected and trusted them absolutely.

'What's all this about?' Barry asked, frowning.

'I need to tell you what I've discovered about Joanne,' I said.

Barry shifted in his seat. 'Nothing you can say will surprise me. I never liked her.'

'This might. As well as having an affair with Troy, she's also had relationships with our clients, Jason Casey, Louis Woods and—'

'Are you sure?' Anthony cut in.

'Positive, I spoke with both of them.'

'God, I wonder how many other clients she's been bothering,' Barry said.

'She's really compromised us.' Anthony looked from me to Barry, frowning.

'I've spoken with Ian who says we are at risk of being sued by Troy for failing in our duty of care.'

'Sued by *Troy?*' Barry interrupted.

'Well, according to Ian, we have a legal obligation to provide a safe work environment,' I said.

Barry began to speak, his voice thick with anger, then thought better of it and said, 'So what does Ian suggest we do?'

'He says we've got no choice but to get rid of Joanne.'

'But how does that solve our problem?' Barry said. 'Troy could still sue us.'

'Yes he could, but we need to cut her loose anyway. She's been with Jason, Louis and Troy and possibly other clients. Who's to say she won't have an affair with another client or employee? Also, getting rid of her sends a signal to all our employees that we won't tolerate sexual impropriety and the abuse of power.'

'Getting her to leave won't be easy. Knowing Joanne, she won't go down without a fight. What does Ian say about how we should approach this?' Anthony asked.

'He says there is an exit procedure and formula to calculate goodwill outlined in the partnership agreement. He's going to draft documents in accordance with the agreement, but if Joanne refuses to sign, we may have to dissolve the partnership.'

'You mean dissolve the business and start from scratch?' Barry said.

'Yes, that's what it comes down to,' I replied.

'That's massive! We'll have to persuade her to sign the documents somehow,' Anthony said.

I sighed. 'I guess I'll have to call her.' I took another deep breath and continued. 'I think I've got the best chance out of all of us to get her to the table.'

⁂

I waited until the new financial year before I called Joanne. The previous night I had lain awake again, remembering the day Joanne came to work with us. I liked her confidence and warmth and thought she would be a great fit for the business. How could so much have changed so quickly?

That morning, before I made the call, I had stood in front of the bathroom mirror and rehearsed what I would say to Joanne.

I hated confrontation and was dreading the conversation, knowing it would be awkward and tricky.

Once I was at my desk I took a deep breath and dialled Joanne's number.

'Joanne, it's Brendan. How are you getting on?'

'Thanks for asking, Brendan. I'm feeling a bit better,' Joanne said hesitantly. 'I took your advice and went to see a psychologist. He's helping me and I'm looking forward to coming back to work.'

I sighed. 'Well, to be brutally honest, Joanne, that's what I'm calling you about. We've spoken with Ian and he says you've put us in a really difficult position with Troy. We need to ensure that our workplace is a safe environment for our employees.'

'I totally understand, Brendan. I'm taking all the necessary steps to rehabilitate myself,' Joanne said, her voice breaking suddenly.

'I'm glad you're getting help but we need to protect the reputation of our business. We need to send a clear signal to our employees that improper behaviour has no place here.'

'So . . . what are you telling me?' Joanne asked.

I hesitated and said, 'You'll get some documents in the next few days that terminate all our financial arrangements.'

'What?'

'Take it easy,' I said softly.

'Look, I've learned my lesson,' Joanne said. 'Please don't do this to me. Can't I have a second chance?'

'Slow down,' I said calmly. 'Why don't you and your lawyer come in for a meeting with the partners and our lawyers to discuss arrangements going forward?'

'Thank you, I appreciate the opportunity,' Joanne said formally and rang off.

A fortnight later, Joanne, grim-faced and ashen, followed Rob, her lawyer, into Ian's boardroom. Barry, Anthony and I were already seated and waiting. Joanne gave me an uncertain smile as she sat down. I shifted in my seat and looked back at her steadily. I felt guilty that I'd lured Joanne to the meeting under false pretences, implying that there might be room for negotiation, knowing full well that it wasn't the case. But it was the only way I could think of to get Joanne to the meeting.

Breaking the heavy silence, Ian looked at Rob and said, 'Let me be clear. We are not here to negotiate. Your client has two choices: if she signs these documents, we'll give her a cheque calculated in accordance with the formula outlined in the partnership agreement. Alternatively, if she chooses not to sign the documents, we will dissolve the partnership and she will get nothing.'

'But hang on, you said we were going to talk about this,' Joanne said, turning to me. The fluorescent lights above the boardroom table reflected on Joanne's glasses, making her face look even paler.

'Joanne,' I said, 'Ian is handling this on our behalf.'

'I can't believe this, Brendan. You've betrayed me!' Joanne said.

'Betrayal, ha! You'd know a thing or two about that, wouldn't you, Joanne?' Barry scoffed.

Rob cut in and said, 'I need to speak with my client. Is there somewhere Joanne and I can have a private conversation?'

'Of course,' Ian said as he directed them to the interview room beyond the large marble reception area.

'Thank you. Give us ten minutes.'

When they left, I turned to Ian and asked, 'Which way do you think this is going to go?'

'If he's smart, Rob will tell her to sign. He'll explain that it's the only way she'll get any money.'

'Were you bluffing about dissolving the partnership?' I asked.

'No. It's not what you want because it will be a lot of work re-establishing the business, but if she doesn't sign, you may have no choice. It's the only way you'll get rid of her.'

'Let's hope she signs,' Anthony said.

There was a knock at the door and Joanne returned with Rob. Joanne's face was impossible to read; I had no idea whether she would sign or not. As they sat down, Joanne's lawyer said, 'It is not our preferred choice, but if there is no option of Joanne staying in the partnership,' he paused for a moment, turning to look at me as I sat rigid in my seat, then continued, 'there seems no choice but to sign.'

Joanne gave me a dark, vindictive look, her mouth clamped shut. She picked up the pen and at the instruction of her lawyer signed the agreement. Her face seemed to have taken on additional lines.

I felt the skin on my arms and on the back of my neck prickle. I let my breath go in a sigh of relief, turned and glanced at my partners, picked up a pen and signed where Ian indicated. I reached into my top pocket, pulled out an envelope and handed the cheque to Joanne's lawyer.

No one said a word. It was as if there had been a death in the family.

As Joanne stood up to leave, I offered her my hand but Joanne turned away and walked out of the room. The tension drained from my body. Finally, the ordeal was over. I hoped never to see Joanne again.

A little over a year later, I was sitting at my desk, head down, working on a file. Through the glass wall I could see my secretary matching Amex receipts with statements and next to her the receptionist was answering and redirecting calls. Troy was lodging annual returns and I could hear the sounds of other accountants at their computers preparing more income tax returns for lodgement. The heavy atmosphere that I associated with Joanne had long gone, although at times I sensed Troy's continuing awkwardness around me.

'Morning,' Barry said, standing in the doorway. 'Are you busy?'

I looked up, startled. 'No, come in.'

'Want to hear some gossip?' Barry said as he sat down.

I nodded. 'Go on,' I said.

'I went to a conference on the weekend and a partner from an accounting firm in Ringwood pulled me aside and told me that our esteemed ex-partner, Joanne, had worked with them for a couple of months. She put them into a dodgy business deal that cost them over a million dollars and now they're suing her.'

After a momentary silence I said, 'Why am I not surprised.'

'So they sacked her. Then she went to a firm in the city, lasted three months and now she's on her own working out of a small room in the outer suburbs. And they told me she separated from her husband, and her kids don't want to know her.'

'She's hopeless, what a loose cannon,' I said. Then after a moment I went on. 'It's actually very sad. You know, she rang my wife to say she was sorry – she said she'd made a mistake. Sarah, sharp as a tack, told her, "When you go to a Christmas party, get drunk and make a pass at a work colleague, that's a mistake. But when you've been having a relationship and concealing it month after month, that's no mistake, that's deliberate."'

❦

Gambling

Bruce came into the kitchen, but before he could speak, Julia said bluntly, 'We got a statement from the bank today. It shows a mortgage of—'

'Julia!' He indicated the boys with a frown, absently resting his briefcase on the table and covering his sons' homework. Ben and Charlie smiled up at him.

'Hi Dad.'

'Hey Dad.'

He gave them a weary grin, but Julia stared pointedly at the case until he moved it. Bruce sighed and said, 'It's been a horrible day.'

'Why didn't you return my calls?' Julia said, checking on a simmering pot. 'I left several messages for you.'

'Don't hassle me.' He stared at the stove, unable to meet her eye.

Julia slapped the lid back on the pot and indicated that he should follow her into the study, out of earshot of the kids.

Bruce slumped into the leather chair behind the desk.

'I'm stuffed.'

Julia opened her mouth to say something but stopped short. Then she said quietly, 'It seems we have a mortgage of nearly a million dollars.'

Bruce started to rock back and forth in his chair, staring at the floor.

'I thought this house was unencumbered!'

Bruce's face was expressionless as he said, 'Julia, let me level with you . . . we're broke.'

Her mouth fell open. 'What?' She steadied herself with one hand on the bookcase. 'What do you mean?'

Bruce shifted uncomfortably in his chair. 'I had to borrow against the house to pay my gambling debts—'

'You're gambling again? Seriously? Since when?'

'It doesn't matter. The bank is going to take possession of the house.'

'We're bankrupt – is that what you're telling me?'

Julia dropped onto the sofa and buried her face in her hands.

'Yes, that's what I'm saying,' Bruce muttered, chewing on his lip.

His wife began to sob, and after a few moments he got up from his chair and sat next to her. He put his arm around her awkwardly and she lifted her head. They locked eyes. 'I'm really sorry,' Bruce said. 'But trust me, everything will be okay.'

Julia wiped her eyes with the back of her hands. 'Everything will be okay?' Her voice was bitter. Over the years she had learnt not to rely on his assurances. 'There is something inside you I don't understand, Bruce,' she said. 'You are a mystery to me. Why on earth didn't you tell me you were gambling again? How could you keep such a thing from me? The last time this happened you promised you would get help . . .' She recalled what she had said to Bruce that last time – that if he continued to gamble, she would leave him. Now she remembered the erratic mood swings, the surliness, the secretiveness, and recognised the signs. She should have known.

'I thought I had it under control,' Bruce mumbled. 'I didn't want to burden you with it. I knew there was nothing you could do.'

Julia removed his arm from her shoulder, shifted sideways and said, 'You should have told me, Bruce. Sometimes I think you live in a world of your own. You lock me out, you don't give a thought to the children and their future. We're supposed to be a team.' Suddenly, she felt overwhelmed: two young children to raise, no home and a useless husband. The future closed against her.

The next morning Julia woke to find Bruce still beside her.

'What are you doing still in bed?' she asked. 'What about work?'

Bruce sat up, leaned heavily against the bedhead and stared blankly out the window. After a few moments he turned towards her and said, 'The liquidator has taken possession of the business.' He hesitated. 'I had to borrow against it as well as the house.'

'You've got to be kidding!' She felt a volcanic rage building inside her. 'What else haven't you told me?' she said through gritted teeth.

'Nothing Julia. There is nothing else.'

She looked at her husband for a long moment and said, 'Don't you think you should go in to work to personally address the staff? There are people who've worked for you for fifteen years. Don't you owe it to them to tell them what's going on?'

'Yes, you're right.' Bruce gave a heavy sigh. 'I'd better tell them.'

Julia lifted the covers, got out of bed and stumbled towards the bathroom. She stepped into the shower and felt as if she were drowning. She thought about all the people she would have to tell about the change in their circumstances: her friends, her family, the kids. Hot waves of shame and anger flushed through her as she grimly contemplated the days ahead.

Julia dropped the boys at school, then drove along Beatty Street, passing the Edwardian homes and overhanging plane trees without seeing them, and soon arrived at her parents' home. They still lived in the house Julia had grown up in and she felt nostalgic for the innocence of her childhood, free of cares and responsibilities.

When Julia let herself in, her mother Margaret was seated at the kitchen table in her floral dressing-gown, eating her usual breakfast of bagel, cream cheese and salmon.

'What's wrong?' Margaret asked as she took in her daughter's pale face and red eyes.

Julia started to speak, but couldn't get the words out. She swallowed hard and took a deep breath. 'It's Bruce,' she said.

'What about him?' Margaret asked, putting down her bagel. 'Has he taken another bad turn?'

Julia hesitated. 'No, it's not his mental health this time, Mum. Yesterday, he told me the business is insolvent. We've lost everything, including the house.'

The fine spidery lines around Margaret's eyes deepened. 'What do you mean, lost everything?' she asked.

'He's been gambling again,' Julia said flatly as she sank onto a kitchen chair.

Margaret started to say something, stopped, then looked away.

'He borrowed against the house and the business to repay his gambling debts and now a liquidator has been appointed to the business and the bank is about to take possession of the house.' Julia heard her words echo in her ears as she spoke.

Margaret sat, stunned, her face pale, her lips quivering.

'I don't know what to do, Mum.'

Margaret turned to her daughter. 'I'm absolutely shocked, Julia. I don't know what to say. Were you aware of the situation?

Did you know how bad things were? Why didn't Brendan warn you?'

'No. Bruce said nothing. You know how closed-off he is. And . . . well, Bruce took all his business to another accountant about three years ago. He said he didn't feel comfortable dealing with family. He asked me not to say anything . . .'

'Oh my goodness, this is awful. You must be so anxious. I think you really should speak to Brendan, whatever Bruce says. Have you told the boys?'

'No, not yet. I thought we'd wait until we worked out what we're going to do,' Julia said, blinking away tears.

'So what *are* you going to do?'

'I don't know, Mum. I don't even know where we are going to live . . .'

'When will you have to move out of the house?'

'Bruce thinks in about three months.'

'I'll talk to your father and Brendan and see what we can do,' Margaret said, getting up and enfolding her daughter in a hug.

'Thanks for your support, Mum. It means a lot to me,' Julia said as she hugged her mother back, then got up to leave.

Julia was sitting at the kitchen table when Bruce got home that night. He kissed her gingerly on the cheek. 'How are you holding up?' he asked.

'With difficulty,' Julia replied. 'I didn't sleep. And I'm still reeling from our conversation last night. But how did it go with the staff?'

'It wasn't easy, but I think they felt for my situation,' Bruce said as he poured himself a whisky and sat down at the kitchen table. 'Want one?'

Julia shook her head.

'I said I'd make some phone calls to see if I could find them work.' He swallowed a mouthful of whisky. 'What did you do? Did you go to work?'

'No, I took the day off and went to see Mum.'

Bruce stiffened. 'Did you tell her about us?'

'Yes, and Mum said she would talk to Dad and Brendan about how they might be able to help us.' As she spoke she noticed the sudden flare of anger in Bruce's eyes.

'Look Julia, I don't want their help,' Bruce said. 'We can work this out ourselves.' He stood up and started pacing around the kitchen. 'Why are you always running to your family to save you?' he hissed. 'You haven't even given me a chance!'

'Can you blame me?' Julia replied. 'You haven't exactly proven yourself to be stable and reliable over the years. This isn't the first time this has happened and you're never honest with me about your gambling. Is it any wonder my trust is at an all-time low?'

'How dare you bring up my mental health issues now!' Bruce said, his eyes burning. 'Where's your compassion, Julia?'

'Don't try to send me on a guilt trip, Bruce. It's your gambling not your illness that's the problem.'

Bruce stopped pacing and stared at her. 'Let me make one thing clear: I do not want your family's money.'

That night, and every night that week, Julia lay awake in bed, worrying about the future and where they would live. Often she would glance over and see that Bruce was also awake, staring up at the ceiling, hands under his head, elbows jutting. He looked thin and worn in the night light, and his face was pale.

At breakfast on Saturday morning, Julia looked at Ben and Charlie, eating their breakfast cereal and watching cartoons.

At ten and twelve, they seemed oddly oblivious to the stress and tension that had been gripping their parents for the past week. It was time to tell them.

Julia began to say something, but then glanced at Bruce, indicating that he should be the one to speak. After all, this was his doing and his reticence made her angry.

Picking up the hint, Bruce turned to the children and said, 'Boys, we might have to move.' He spoke mechanically, without emotion, and Julia had the feeling he wasn't talking so much to the children as to himself.

Ben glanced at his father, puzzled. 'Why?'

There was a long moment of silence during which Ben and his father gazed at each other. Finally Julia spoke. 'Dad's had some problems at work and we have to sell the house.'

'Will we have to change schools?' Charlie asked, small frown lines appearing on his forehead.

'Maybe,' Julia said as she walked over and put her arms around him.

Later that day, after she'd dropped the boys at football, she came home and found Bruce still in his pyjamas. 'Come on, let's go for a walk. It's time you got dressed. I need to talk to you.'

They headed towards the bike track that ran beside the river. Bruce looked surly and resentful, shoulders hunched, hands jammed in his pockets.

Julia hesitated for a moment before speaking. 'Bruce?'

He refused to look at her.

'Bruce, Dad rang this morning while I was out. He's offered to buy back the house from the bank – but only if it's in my name.' As she said the words she felt her heart pounding and the blood rushing in her ears.

Bruce stopped short, turning to look at Julia in alarm. 'What did you say?'

'Before you question me, Bruce, tell me this: if we don't accept Dad's offer, where do you suggest we live? You heard the kids at breakfast; I really don't want them to have to move schools.'

'I knew it! You can't help yourself, can you?' Bruce said, his voice rising. 'I knew you'd accept his offer.'

'Bruce, take it easy. It gives me no pleasure to realise that we are again in the same position. What do you expect from me? Think of the kids . . .'

Bruce shook his head and marched off. Running to catch up with him Julia called, 'I just don't get it, Bruce. I'm trying to understand. My parents love us, they love the kids and they love being with us; that's why they want to help us.'

Bruce stopped and turned to her. 'No they don't. They want to help you, that's why they want the house in your name. I told you once, and I'll tell you again, I don't want their money. I hate feeling indebted to them.' He glared at her. 'They would always remind me of what we owe them.'

Julia sighed. 'I'm sorry you feel that way, Bruce, but my parents have always acted out of love and concern for us and the kids. They don't hold it over us; they've never once asked to be repaid for the help they gave us when we were down and out the first time.'

'They don't say it, Julia, but I feel it.'

'Perhaps that's coming from you,' Julia said, her eyes hardening. 'But it seems nothing I say will convince you.'

Bruce shrugged but said nothing.

'With you, they can't win. If they don't help us, you'll say they're mean, but if they do help us, you'll resent it.'

'They make demands on us and I feel obliged to comply.'

Julia's tired eyes grew wide with astonishment. 'What demands?'

Bruce put on a mincing voice: 'Can we take the kids for the weekend, can we do this, can we do that . . . it's never-ending.'

Julia realised there was nothing more she could say. He was like the needle of a record-player stuck in the same groove, playing the same phrase over and over.

That afternoon Julia was putting glasses away in the cabinet in the living room when she noticed the empty space on the buffet where her parents' photo usually stood. She went straight to the living room where Bruce was playing video games, as he had been doing for the past week.

'Bruce, where's the photo of my parents that was always on the buffet?'

Bruce continued to play, his eyes on the screen. 'I'm done with that photo.'

'Why did you move it? Where did you put it?'

Bruce finally turned to face her and said, 'I've had enough of your parents.'

'Bruce!' she shouted. 'Put down the controller. Look at me. Talk to me. What is your problem?'

Bruce threw the controller to the floor and said, 'My problem is your parents. They're in my face, all day, every minute of every day – visiting whenever it suits them, dropping in for dinner. I feel like I'm suffocating in my own home; they don't give us any space.'

'Don't be ridiculous!' Julia said. 'I've had it with you! I'm going to get the boys from school.' She grabbed the car keys and her bag, a choking thickness in her throat as she got into the car.

When she arrived at school, the boys came pelting towards her with two friends, brothers they particularly liked. 'Can we have a sleepover with Finn and Rupe?' Ben said. 'Their dad says it's fine. And we don't need stuff. We can borrow theirs. Can we Mum, please?'

'Why not,' Julia said with a sigh.

Julia pulled over on her way home and sat staring vacantly out over the bay. She was glad the boys were somewhere else tonight. She and Bruce needed to really talk, but about what? What could they do? She felt helpless in the face of this disaster, weighed down by all she would have to do, all they would have to endure, and Bruce seemed paralysed . . . Finally she noticed the sun was setting and a sea mist was gathering. She started the car and drove home.

Bruce was still sitting in the same seat in the living room, now staring vacantly at the TV screen. 'Bruce, look at me,' she said.

He raised his head slowly and turned towards her. Julia saw his eyes were wet.

'I want to say something. It hurts me to be caught between you and my parents, but this can't continue,' she said.

Bruce rubbed the side of his face. 'Why do they always turn up unannounced?' he asked in a thin voice.

'That's what grandparents do.' Julia could see Bruce wavering between his pain and acknowledgment of Julia's point of view.

He seemed not to know what to say. 'Bruce, you're looking for someone to blame. Don't make them your scapegoats. It's all wrong. What are we going to do? Where are we going to live?'

Bruce looked out the window at the darkening sky, turned back to Julia and murmured, 'I don't know.'

'Let's just talk to my parents, eh?'

Bruce was silent, his shoulders bowed, then he muttered, 'What for? I know what your father will say.'

'What? What will he say?'

'I gave you money and now this is how you treat us.'

'No he won't. That's not how he thinks.'

Bruce looked at Julia intently. 'If he doesn't say it, he'll think it.'

'Bruce, we're getting nowhere, this is ridiculous. We need help. We need to speak with them. What choice do we—'

There was a knock at the door. Bruce's face went rigid, then his expression slipped into a knowing smile, as if to say, *I knew it.*

Julia felt her stomach clench. She stared at Bruce, then looked quickly away and went to answer the door.

'Come in, we're in the living room.' Julia led her parents into the room and saw Bruce grimace as they entered.

'Ron. Margaret.' He barely managed to say their names.

'Sit down,' Julia said. 'I'll make you a coffee.'

'Coffee would be good,' Ron said.

'We were just talking about you,' Julia said when she returned with the coffee and handed her parents a mug each. She turned towards Bruce and nodded, encouraging him to speak.

Bruce sat up straighter in his chair, then after a moment's silence said, 'Firstly, thank you for your offer to buy back the house.

I know Julia really appreciates it.' He sighed. 'Look, I wish we weren't in this position, but we have little choice but to accept your offer. I want you to know, though, that I feel very uncomfortable about it.'

'Uncomfortable? Why?' Margaret asked, confused.

Julia's father sipped his coffee and looked at his son-in-law. Before Bruce could answer, Ron put down his mug and said, 'Seeing we are being honest, let me say a couple of things. We find you very inconsistent Bruce. Some days you barely speak, then at other times you're warm and engaged. We never know where we stand with you.'

Bruce was silent, his mouth slightly open.

'We gave Julia her inheritance early. She needed it because of the mess you'd put your family in.'

Bruce winced.

'You have a wife and kids. You need to stop gambling, stop hiding behind your so-called mental health issues and accept your obligations.'

Bruce was silent. His failure to offer an apology or even a response made Ron angry. He was a gentle, compassionate man, but he could not understand how his son-in-law could behave in such an irresponsible way. 'Frankly, why Julia chooses to stay with you is beyond me – but that's her choice.' His eyes were blazing now. 'For my part, I'm not prepared to risk giving you any more money, that's why I will only buy back the house in Julia's name. I am not prepared to entrust you with the property again.'

Julia stared at her husband, sighed and turned away. Without a word, Bruce pushed his chair back and left the room.

Julia felt the blood drain from her face. She looked at her parents and said, 'I can't do this anymore – I'm done.'

Margaret glanced from her husband to her daughter to the door through which Bruce had just left. She looked utterly baffled.

'Julia?' Ron said, his eyes fixed on his daughter.

'Thanks, Dad,' she said. 'I'll accept your kind offer, and your conditions. Bruce can make his own way. The boys and I need a home.'

The Will

The doorbell rang.

'Come in, it's open,' Helen called. She slid the chocolate cake onto the glass-topped dining table beside the coffee cups. Not that she thought anyone would eat it.

It was five in the afternoon, a cold, cloudy winter's day. Sophie walked into the dining room clutching a wet umbrella and shoved it behind the door. Her younger sister Laura was close behind, still wearing her white lab coat, a lanyard strung around her neck. She must have come straight from work, Helen thought. Unlike Sophie, she seemed relaxed and composed: no frown lines on her forehead, no puffiness around her eyes.

Sophie made a beeline for her mother and fell into her arms. 'Give me a hug,' she said, 'I've had a shocking day.'

Helen noted the thin, drawn face, the dark circles under her eyes, and the uncharacteristically casual tracksuit top and black leggings. She wrapped her arms around Sophie in a tight embrace and said soothingly, 'Don't worry, everything will sort itself out.' Stepping back, she looked more closely at her and asked, 'What have you done to your hair?'

'Oh, I decided to cut it. I can't be bothered with long hair anymore.'

'I like it,' Laura said. 'It suits you.'

'It's practical,' Sophie said flatly. She seemed distracted and unsettled.

'How are you feeling about today, Mum?' Laura asked.

'I'm nervous,' Helen said, her husky voice cracking a little.

Laura moved towards her mother and kissed her on the cheek. 'Don't worry,' she said. 'Nanna may have been a bit demented these last few years, but she was sensible and fair.'

Laura turned towards Sophie. 'So, how are things with you? How are the kids getting on?'

'It's been hell, actually,' Sophie said. 'Spencer wants to go and live with Jack, and Charlotte is being bullied at school. And Jack has been a nightmare.'

'Why am I not surprised?' Laura mumbled.

Sophie gave her sister a sharp look, then continued, 'He promises to pick the kids up from school then just doesn't turn up; says he'll give me money then complains he doesn't have any . . . it's been horrible.'

'But he's a successful merchant banker,' Laura said. 'Surely he has to pay you maintenance?'

'He says he lost all our money trading the market and now we have to sell the house to pay down the mortgage,' Sophie said.

'I never trusted him; I bet he has hidden assets,' Laura said. 'He'll do everything he can to wriggle out of his obligations.'

Sophie stared at Laura for a moment, leaned forward to speak, then hesitated.

'But can't some of your rich friends help?' Laura went on.

'And what's that supposed to mean?' Sophie snapped.

'Now is not the time for bickering,' Helen said. 'Cut it out.'

The doorbell rang at just the right time.

'Alan, come in,' Helen said, standing back to let him pass. 'I'd like you to meet my daughters, Sophie, and Laura.'

Alan King extended his hand to the women, who had followed their mother to the door. 'We've not met,' he said. 'I'm your grandmother's executor. I was Clara's solicitor and confidant for over twenty years.'

'Come, let's move into the dining room,' Helen suggested as she ushered Alan down the hallway. He had aged since Helen last saw him. A short man with a round face and heavy, black-rimmed glasses, he had even less hair now. Today he was wearing a dark jacket but no tie, his white shirt open at the collar.

'At the outset, let me say that I am sorry for your loss,' Alan began after they had settled themselves around the table. 'I was very fond of your grandmother.' He reached into his briefcase and pulled out a manila file. 'I don't intend to read the whole Will, just those parts that are relevant to each of you.'

Opening the file, he looked at Laura and began to read:
'I bequeath free of all duties to my granddaughter Laura Benson my family home located at 17A St Georges Road, Toorak, as an expression of my gratitude for her love and support.'

He paused for a moment, then turned to Sophie. 'I bequeath to my granddaughter Sophie Turner my wedding ring and my engagement ring as an expression of my gratitude for her love and support.'

Helen felt a sudden pounding inside her head and a pressure in her chest. She took a deep breath, but the tension remained. Outside, the trees looked battered and forlorn in the winter rain.

When Alan King indicated that Clara's home had recently been valued at $3.5 million, Laura's mouth fell open and she shifted in her seat. When he explained that the rings had been valued at $75,000, Sophie's face blanched and she blinked a few times in disbelief.

Helen looked at Alan questioningly, trying to grapple with what he had just said.

'What about Mum?' Sophie stammered.

'She is not included,' he said matter-of-factly, his face showing no emotion.

'But why not? That doesn't make sense,' Laura said.

'Clara was my mother-in-law, not my mother,' Helen interrupted, looking at Laura. 'I didn't expect to be included in the Will.'

'But after everything you did for her, it's not fair—'

'It's not my place to question the reasons behind my client's wishes,' Alan interjected. 'My job is to document them.'

He paused momentarily before continuing, 'Do you have any further questions?'

After a moment's silence Helen said, 'Alan, I think we need some time to absorb what you've said.'

'Of course. I'll organise probate, and should you have any questions, please feel free to contact me,' Alan said, standing up to leave.

'Thank you for coming out,' Helen said as she walked him to the door. The coffee things and chocolate cake were untouched.

When Helen returned to the dining room, she felt shaken to her core.

'You look as bad as I feel,' Sophie muttered.

'I am absolutely stunned,' Helen said. 'I just don't know what to make of this . . .'

'Well, it's pretty obvious,' Sophie said. 'Nanna must have made her Will when I was still married to Jack and living in Brighton.'

She paused. 'God, how quickly life changes.'

'Yes, I guess so,' Helen said, then turned to Laura. 'And because you were on a research grant, Nanna must have thought you were in financial difficulties.'

'Well, I was. And I'm still struggling,' Laura said. 'I live from one grant to the next.'

'Anyway, the question is: what do we do now?' Sophie said.

'Well, the Will is very clear,' Laura said cautiously. 'There is no ambiguity. We must simply respect Nanna's wishes.'

The lines in Sophie's face deepened. 'Hang on a minute. How can you accept that this is fair? You get a house in Toorak and I get a couple of rings? Seriously?'

'I'm not saying it's fair,' Laura said, 'but it is what it is. And in any case,' she continued, her voice rising, 'for the past ten years you've been living the high life: overseas trips twice a year, holiday house down the coast, live-in maids and nannies and private schools . . . it's only now, since Jack left, that you bother to pick up the phone and call me. And then only when you need something. Where were you when I was forced to move out of my apartment and find somewhere cheaper to live?'

Sophie clenched her jaw but said nothing. Her pupils were large and dark and a red flush was spreading across her face and neck.

'Back then you didn't want to know me,' Laura said. 'So maybe this is karma.'

Sophie stared at her sister in disbelief. 'I don't have to listen to this,' she said. 'I'm leaving.'

'I'll ring you tomorrow,' Helen called.

Sophie strode down the corridor and slammed the door behind her.

Laura stood at the dining-room window and gazed out at the bare magnolia tree. Turning to look at her mother, she said, 'You probably think I should give Sophie half the house, don't you?'

'Oh, I don't know,' Helen said with a sigh. 'Look, I realise how much you've struggled over the years and I know that Sophie has never offered to help you. She's been very neglectful and selfish . . . But I'd hate to see the two of you falling out over this.'

Laura shook her head in disbelief. 'Mum, you're living in a fantasy world. My relationship with Sophie dissolved the moment she married that idiot Jack and became obsessed with nothing but wealth and status.'

'But what will happen to her now?'

'Sophie is not my responsibility, Mum. And do you really think she's going to walk away from this divorce with nothing?'

'There's nothing left – Sophie is looking for work.'

Laura shrugged. 'Also, please remember that I did not make this Will. I'm simply saying that we should abide by Nanna's wishes.'

The following morning Helen wandered through the silent rooms of her home, stopping for a moment to look into the girls' bedroom. Where would this crisis take them? She was sure her heart would break if her daughters were estranged.

She remembered Laura sitting at her desk studying for her final exams – she was always such a diligent student – and now research was her life. Then she recalled Sophie dressing for her high-school formal in the two-thousand-dollar dress she'd pressured her father into buying. Poor Robert. At least he hadn't lived to see this.

If Helen were honest, she'd always known the girls were not close; their values and priorities could not have been more different.

The sound of the doorbell broke her reverie. Wondering who it could be, she hurried to answer it.

'Oh, it's you,' she said to Sophie. 'Where are the children?'

'At school,' Sophie said, blinking back tears.

'Darling, what's wrong?'

'I couldn't sleep last night – just kept tossing and turning and brooding over what Laura said. Eventually I gave up and went to the kitchen to make a cup of tea.'

'Oh darling . . .'

'I thought about all the stupid misguided decisions I've made: marrying Jack, living extravagantly, neglecting my family. How did I end up so selfish? So obsessed with money? Maybe Nanna's Will really is karma, like Laura said. Maybe these are my just deserts.'

'Darling, I—'

'Then this morning I spoke with a lawyer friend and told him about the Will,' Sophie went on in a choked voice. 'He doesn't think I should challenge. He doesn't know that I'd be successful or not, and the cost of trying would be prohibitive.'

Helen looked at her daughter and frowned.

'He suggested I talk to Laura—'

'No, don't do that,' Helen said. 'Not just yet. Let me speak to her. Leave it to me, I'll talk to her.'

⁀

'Laura, it's me,' Helen said as she paced the hallway gripping the phone. 'Can I come and see you?'

'Of course you can, Mum. But if it's about Nanna's Will, there's nothing to say.'

Helen felt her face go hot. 'That's not true, Laura. We have a lot to talk about.'

'Look, I feel bad for Sophie. I know she's upset and I know she's vulnerable. But as I've said already: we need to respect Nanna's wishes.'

'Hang on. Do you believe that if Nanna had known Sophie would be left high and dry by a cheating husband she would have made the same Will?'

'Nobody knows the answer to that, Mum. We can only deal with the facts.'

Helen rolled her eyes. Always the facts with Laura. 'But what about your relationship with your sister?' she pleaded. 'This could have long-term repercussions . . .'

'Well, that's Sophie's choice. It's up to her how she responds to this. She needs to decide whether she accepts Nanna's wishes or not. A Will is a Will.'

'Listen to me,' Helen said firmly. 'Family matters. I don't want trouble between you and your sister.'

'Neither do I,' Laura bit back. 'So talk to Sophie.'

The following morning, Helen woke early, made her usual breakfast of tea, toast and marmalade and sat watching the clock. As it struck nine, she picked up the phone and rang her accountant.

'It's Helen,' she said. 'Brendan, I want to change my Will. Can I come to your office today? I need to discuss my plans with someone I trust before I see my solicitor.'

'Yes, of course, Helen. How about three this afternoon?'

Later that day, Brendan ushered Helen into his office. 'Can I get you a coffee? Tea?'

'No thanks, Brendan. I had a coffee while I was waiting.'

'Right, well, give me a heads up: what do you want to do?' Brendan asked.

Helen took a deep breath. 'I want to compensate Sophie somehow for her grandmother's Will,' she said, and went on to explain the details of the Will and what she had in mind.

Brendan was silent a long time, then he said, 'You mean, you want to leave Sophie more than Laura?'

'Yes, that's exactly what I mean, and I want to know if I can afford to do it sooner rather than later.'

'Be careful,' Brendan cautioned.

'Why?'

'Well, circumstances may change; and secondly, if you leave Laura less, she may think you loved Sophie more. People often misinterpret these things.'

'Oh Brendan, what do I do?' Helen cried. 'We're on the brink of a major war here!'

Brendan thought for a moment, then said, 'Why don't you tell the girls that you intend to divide your estate equally, rather than giving Sophie more, but that you'll give Sophie her inheritance now, as you suggested, and Laura will get hers upon your death?'

As Helen absorbed the implications of Brendan's proposal, she felt the tension drain from her body. Sophie would be all right. The sisters could move beyond this trouble and perhaps grow close again.

'Brendan, you have the wisdom of Solomon,' she said. 'I can't thank you enough.'

'All part of the service,' he replied. 'Now, let's go through your assets and you can decide what you want to sell or transfer to Sophie.'

Tuscany

It was a warm Saturday afternoon. The sky was clear and sun streamed through the window onto the rumpled sheets. Chloe lay gazing up at Joe, her head in the crook of his shoulder, his arm around her.

'You're different from my other clients,' she said, smiling at him. 'In my business, you see them all – salesmen, corporate types, tradies, academics . . .'

'How am I different?' Joe asked.

'You like to talk. You listen to what I've got to say and you don't seem preoccupied with sex all the time.'

He raised one eyebrow.

'No, I don't mean—' She hesitated. 'Maybe I shouldn't tell you this but I enjoy being with you.'

He returned her look, smiled, but said nothing.

'And you're not weird. One of my clients insists I dress as a schoolgirl – short dress, frilly white socks, ribbons, no underwear. He forces me to bend over so he can take me from behind.
I always shower straight after he leaves but I never feel clean.'

'Creep.' Joe was thoughtful for a minute, then he said, 'What do you do for security? Are you ever afraid?'

'A few years ago I met an older bloke who took a liking to me, so we teamed up. He drives me to my clients and waits downstairs in the car. If I get into trouble I stand at the window. I pay him for his time and once a week I service him. It works well.'

'Is he outside now?'

Chloe laughed. 'What do you think?'

'I'm glad there's someone looking out for you,' Joe said.

'Hey, I saw you on TV last night.' Chloe raised herself on one elbow. 'You were standing outside the court with a client, that guy who—'

'Was I talking to the press?'

'Yes, and you looked very distinguished.' She patted his chest. 'Nice crisp white shirt, and that red tie with the perfect Windsor knot. You looked great.'

'Gotta look the part,' he said.

They lay in silence for a while, until finally he said, 'I need to talk to you about something important, Chloe.'

'What is it?'

'On second thoughts, maybe now's not the time. There are a few things I need to take care of first.'

Chloe got out of bed and walked to the window. They were on the second floor of Joe's penthouse, with a view over the lake. She loved this place, loved the view. She turned back to Joe but he had got out of bed and was pulling on his suit pants. The dark navy suit, with its bright red handkerchief in the breast pocket, was hanging neatly on the chair next to the door.

'I won't see you next week, Chloe, I'm going overseas,' Joe said, doing up his fly.

'I guessed as much. You go overseas pretty regularly, don't you.'

'Yeah.'

There was something closed-off about Joe. He was particularly evasive about his overseas travel, and she had learned not to ask him about where he'd been or what he'd done. Today, he seemed tense but she didn't push him. He might tell her when the time was right.

The following day Chloe decided to give her apartment a good clean, ruminating on her conversation with Joe. What had he wanted to tell her, she wondered. He was getting married . . . he already had a wife . . . She plugged in the vacuum cleaner. He was planning to move overseas . . . he had some dreadful disease . . . no, not that. Joe wanted to tell her he was in love with her, wanted her to stop working and come and live with him.

She played out the fantasy as she cleaned, elaborating, modifying, adding details until she knew exactly what kind of wedding they'd have, where they'd live, and how many children they'd have.

In the six years she'd been doing sex work, Chloe had never felt such a connection with a client. Perhaps she was in love with him. She tried cautioning herself against this wishful thinking – she knew it was rare for a working relationship to develop into something more enduring – but she couldn't help hoping, and what harm was there in a bit of fantasy. If it was good enough for her clients it was good enough for her.

Feeling tired that evening, Chloe ran a bath. She missed Joe and hoped his week away would go quickly. As she lay in the warm scented water she returned to her fantasy about their future together. Joe would be the one to take her away from the dirty men, the parlours and the prostitution. Together they would start life afresh – children, a house in a leafy street, and morning tea with the neighbours. But most of all, a husband who loved her.

The phone rang. 'I've just got in. Maybe we can go for a walk?'

It was Joe.

'I'd like that.'

'I'll pick you up in an hour.'

At eleven o'clock, Joe pulled up outside her apartment, his black Porsche glistening in the morning sun.

After driving in silence for a few minutes he said, 'How long have we been seeing each other? About four months?'

'At least,' Chloe said.

'You know, I was thinking that I still don't know much about you.'

Chloe was flattered. No client had ever expressed much interest in her, beyond the services she could provide.

They arrived at the park and strolled along the path towards the lake. Joe had brought some bread for the ducks, and Chloe was touched by his thoughtfulness. They sat on a wooden bench in the sun and tossed crusts to some black ducks.

'I've never told anybody my story,' Chloe said. She gave Joe a careful look. 'What is it you want to know about me?'

'Well, for starters, tell me about your family.'

'I'm an only child. My father is a barrister and my mother's a GP . . .'

'A barrister? I probably know him.'

'I don't have any contact with my parents,' Chloe said quickly.

'You're estranged.'

'You could say that,' Chloe said flatly, turning to gaze out over the lake.

'Why? What happened?' Joe asked.

Chloe collected herself before she spoke. She was glad he didn't press her for details, but waited patiently until she was ready. 'When I was a little girl my father abused me. It continued until I turned fifteen.'

Joe looked appalled.

'If my mother had been less concerned about her patients and more concerned about me, she would have been there to protect me.'

Joe pulled her close. 'That's awful, Chloe. I'm so sorry,' he said softly. 'Did you ever tell your mum about what your father was doing?'

'No, never.'

'Why not? You should have said something.'

'I didn't think she'd believe me.'

The lake darkened as a cloud covered the sun and the ducks squawked and bickered over crumbs.

Chloe pressed on: may as well tell it all. 'When I was eighteen I fell pregnant. My parents, who are Catholic, were more concerned about the shame of an unmarried pregnancy than what I was going through. I remember thinking, *Fuck you! What would your precious friends say if they knew I'd been raped by my father?*' Her eyes were dark and her voice trembled as she spoke.

'I wanted to have the baby, get married, but my parents didn't approve of my boyfriend and forced me to have an abortion. I've never forgiven them for that.'

Chloe paused, glanced at Joe and saw that he was staring out over the water, his lips pressed together. He was utterly still.

'I couldn't live with them anymore, so I left. I had no money and nowhere to go, but I had to get out of there.'

'So what did you do?'

'I moved in with a friend.'

'But how did you support yourself?'

'At first I tried waitressing but it didn't cover my rent, let alone my other expenses. Then a girl I knew suggested I do sex work. I laughed at her, but then I started to consider it. After all, it couldn't be worse than what I'd already endured.

'So I changed my name and placed an advertisement in the local newspaper. It wasn't long before I had a regular clientele.'

Joe looked at Chloe for a long time. 'That's some story,' he said, shaking his head.

'Now it's your turn,' Chloe said. 'Tell me about you. All I know is you're a lawyer, you've got lots of celebrity clients, and for some mysterious reason you travel overseas pretty regularly. It sounds crazy, but I don't even know if you're married.'

'No, never married, no kids. Never met the right woman,' Joe said, shrugging.

Chloe felt her heart lift. 'Maybe your future bride is closer than you think,' Chloe said, giving him a mischievous grin.

He laughed, then looked away. He seemed deep in thought and she worried that she'd overstepped the mark.

'Are your parents still around?' Chloe asked.

'Yes, both retired. They still live in the house they bought when they first came to Australia.'

'Where did they come from?'

'Poland.'

'What work did they do?'

'My mother was a schoolteacher before coming to Australia, but she had to work as a cleaner. And my father, an engineer, could only get work as a linesman on the railway,' Joe said. 'They've had it really tough.'

He smiled then and said, 'But soon I'll be able to buy them a mansion in Toorak, or anywhere else they'd like to live.'

It was Chloe's turn to laugh. Just for a moment he'd sounded like a proud little boy. 'Did you always want to be a lawyer?' she asked.

'For my parents, education was everything; they wanted me to go to uni and become a professional – a doctor, a lawyer, either would do.' He grinned. 'And because of their wartime experience, and their communism, I've always been drawn to social-justice issues. I wanted to do some good in the world. Law seemed the best way to do it.'

'That's pretty impressive,' Chloe said. Not only was Joe tall and distinguished, he was a good person with a social conscience.

After a while she said, 'I don't want you to pay me anymore, Joe.'

'Why not?' he asked, taken aback.

'Because I enjoy being with you. It doesn't feel like work.'

'But you need to make a living, and I have plenty of money,' he said. He took her hand then glanced at his watch. 'Much as I'd love to keep talking, Chloe, I'd better go. I have to meet a client.'

He got to his feet and Chloe walked beside him, hand in hand. She'd hoped to ask him what he'd wanted to talk to her about, but the conversation had taken an unexpected turn. On the way back to her flat, they barely spoke, each lost in thought.

Chloe came to Joe's apartment, as usual, the following week. As they lay in bed gazing at the rain trickling down the window, Chloe lifted her head and asked softly, 'What was it you wanted to tell me the other day? You said it was important.'

'Not now,' Joe said soothingly. 'When the time's right I'll tell you.'

He stood up, walked to the other side of the room, picked up the remote control and turned on the TV. 'I think I'll be on the six o'clock news,' he said.

'How come?'

'One of my clients was accused of fraud and I managed to get him off on a technicality.'

'Really?'

'Yeah, they had him tied up tight, the auditor was unassailable, but the Crown overlooked one critical detail. They accused him of fraudulently obtaining an exact amount, rather than a range, and then they couldn't present evidence to prove it.' He laughed.

'If I ever get into trouble with the law you'll be the man for me,' Chloe said, her face breaking into a smile.

'And if you ever need a good accountant, I can give you the name of the guy who went through my client with a fine-tooth comb. Brendan Baer – impressive, but in the event, not enough to nail him.' Joe shrugged.

Chloe gazed at him admiringly. After a long moment, he said, 'How would you like to come to Tuscany with me? Start life afresh?'

Chloe stared at him, 'What? Do you mean . . . leave Australia and go and live in Italy?'

'Sure. You've got nothing holding you back: no family ties, no children – why not?'

Chloe looked at Joe's handsome face. It was true; there was nothing holding her to Australia and she had always longed for a fresh start, a chance to live the kind of life she felt she deserved. She nodded, smiled uncertainly and felt a tremor of excitement move through her. Her heart began to beat faster. 'I'd love to,' she said. 'Are you sure? Really?'

'I'm sure,' he said. 'That's wonderful, Chloe, I'm so pleased.' He came back to the bed and folded her in his arms. 'I just have to tie up a few loose ends, which will take a couple of weeks,' he said. 'I'm going overseas again in a few weeks and I can finalise everything then. We'll plan to leave a month after I return, if that gives you enough time?' He leaned over and kissed her on the cheek.

*

That night Chloe lay back on her pillow, staring up at the ceiling, her palms under her head. For the first time in years she thought about her father and what he had done to her; she thought about her work and how she hated it; but most of all she thought about Joe: his chiselled face, his good looks, his sophistication, his kindness. And she thought about Tuscany. Would she be able to sleep with so much to think about and so many plans?

*

The next morning Chloe woke and turned on the news.

'A prominent Melbourne lawyer has been charged with drug trafficking,' the journalist said. 'Joseph Malik, a respected corporate lawyer, was charged overnight with trafficking heroin and other narcotics after an undercover operation targeting drug trafficking between Australia and Italy. According to police, Malik developed a global network of prostitutes whom he persuaded to act as drug mules.'

Chloe started to shake. When the broadcast ended she jumped up from her chair and grabbed the remote to see whether the story was being run on another channel. She sat down again, staring in disbelief at the television. This couldn't be true. Surely there was an explanation – a case of mistaken identity, or . . .

She threw on a tracksuit and headed for the door. She needed to do something, to clear her head, to think about what she'd just heard. As she strode along the footpath she thought about Joe and the months they'd been seeing each other. In all the time she'd known him, he had never really revealed himself to her. He was very evasive, always watching from behind that two-way mirror in his head. It was starting to make sense, his other business, the one he had never told her about. The regular overseas trips must have been to do with importing drugs.

One question kept nagging at her, although she hated to think about it. Did he intend to coerce her into becoming a part of his network of prostitutes? Her head began to spin and she stopped walking. Had she been living in a parallel universe to Joe, deluded into thinking she actually meant something to him when in fact he was setting her up to be another pawn in his game?

She felt tears on her cheeks as she took her phone from her pocket and tapped in a number.

'Crystal it's me, Chloe,' she said, her voice trembling.

'What's wrong honey?'

'Have you seen the news this morning?'

'No, I'm still in bed. Why?'

'My client – Joe – has been arrested for drug trafficking!'

'Joe? Your regular? That lawyer?'

'Yes. Just yesterday he asked me to go to Tuscany with him. I think he planned to use me as a drug mule.' There, she'd said it.

'That bastard. All men are bastards,' Crystal said matter-of-factly.

'I get it wrong every time,' Chloe said, wiping her eyes with the back of her hand. 'I was so stupid. I suspected he was hiding something from me but I kept telling myself he was entitled to, he was a client, not a boyfriend. And I didn't want to believe it.

I was in love with him and I fooled myself into thinking he felt the same way about me. What an idiot.'

'That rotten son of a bitch; I'm really sorry, babe,' Crystal said. 'Call me if you need to talk. Gotta go.'

Chloe turned off her phone and stood for a minute, trying to calm herself. She felt the shock turning to rage. She wanted to hit him, smash him, kill him, so she would never have to see his face, listen to his empty promises, ever again.

The next morning Chloe sat in gloomy silence at the kitchen bench, a cup of coffee cooling at her elbow. She had lain awake a long time last night, unable to sleep. She mulled over her times with Joe, everything he'd said, all the hints he'd dropped.

She needed to confront him. She couldn't let him slide away like a snake without giving her some sort of explanation. She needed to know if he'd really loved her. She wanted to shout at him, 'I loved you!'

At nine o'clock she took a deep breath, picked up the phone and rang the Melbourne Remand Centre.

'Are you holding Joe Malik?'

'Who am I speaking to?' the woman at the other end said.

'I'm his sister,' Chloe said after a momentary pause.

'Yes, we have him.'

'I need to see him, is that possible?' she asked.

'Not today. He's being questioned. Come in tomorrow.'

When Chloe arrived at the Remand Centre the following morning, she was led through a heavy metal door, down a corridor and into a small, dimly lit room. The bare walls and grey floor were grim, reflecting the emptiness she felt inside. Set high in the wall opposite the door was a narrow window with iron bars across it.

Chloe wondered what kind of room Joe was being held in. She imagined a small cell with a moth-eaten blanket, a filthy mattress and a bucket in the corner, but that was only in the movies. This place looked pretty new. She struggled to reconcile the sophisticated, urbane man she had come to know with this dismal room. She wanted to cry.

Chloe took a seat at the table. Silence seemed to press against the walls, against her head, her ears. She waited.

After a few minutes Joe was escorted into the room by a man in uniform. Looking exhausted, his pale face unshaven, his hair uncombed, he sat down heavily opposite her. He avoided her eyes and fixed his gaze at a point above her head.

'Well?' she said, when he continued to ignore her. 'What's going on, Joe?'

He shifted uncomfortably in his seat, kept his gaze averted and refused to speak.

Losing patience, Chloe banged her fist on the table. 'Talk to me, Joe! You owe me that much.'

Still he didn't move, his face blank.

'Was I intended to be one of your drug mules?' she hissed.

Joe leaned back in his chair and dropped his eyes to where he fiddled with the edge of the table. He still steadfastly refused to look at her.

Chloe let the silence lengthen, then she sighed. 'You're selfish and you use people,' she said, standing up. 'You're just like my father.'

Henshaw Family Business

A guttural screech came from reception. I lifted my head from my ledgers, but before I could get up from the desk, Alison Kavanagh barged into my office, hastily followed by my secretary. While my client ranted, Jane fluttered about trying to quieten her, reminding her she was in an accountant's office.

'Alison, what a surprise. I wasn't aware you had an appointment this morning,' I said.

Alison was dressed in black leggings and a turquoise kaftan, and she was clearly extremely angry. She removed her glasses, wiped her eyes with the back of her hand, replaced the glasses and took a deep breath. 'I don't, but this is urgent.' She looked pointedly at Jane who glanced at me, then left.

'I desperately need to talk to you,' Alison said.

'Okay, sit down. Can I get you some water or a coffee?'

She slumped into a chair and flicked her long black hair from her face, her bangles jangling. 'Actually, if you've got a joint it'd help.'

I smiled. 'Sorry, that falls beyond my purview.' I poured her a glass of water from the carafe on my desk. 'Tell me what's upsetting you.'

She began to speak, then stopped and took a deep breath. 'It's my . . . fucking brother . . .'

I was taken aback by the violence of her language.

'I didn't get my monthly payment, Brendan.'

'Maybe he forgot to make the payment this month.'

'In the fifteen years I have been receiving monthly distributions from the family business, Shaun has never once missed a payment. Anyway, I rang him.'

'And what did he say?'

'He mumbled something about banks, liquidity problems, liquidation, blah, blah, blah, but I didn't understand what the hell he was talking about.'

'So how did the conversation end?'

'How it always ends with him – nowhere. I just slammed the phone down.'

'Alison, do you want me to talk to your brother and find out what's going on?'

'Yes, better you speak to him than I do, Brendan. The less I have to do with him the better. To be honest, I was done with him years ago.'

'Okay, leave it with me, Alison.' I stood up and walked her to the door.

As she reached the corridor she turned and grabbed my hand. 'I need you to sort this for me, Brendan. I'm dependent on that money.'

I reassured her that I'd do all I could to help, then sat down at my desk, my head spinning. Jane knocked on the door. 'Sorry about that, Brendan. I tried to stop her but she was like a force of nature.'

'Don't worry about it, Jane, it's fine. But please arrange a meeting with Shaun Henshaw for some time tomorrow.'

I tried to concentrate on my ledgers – debits and credits, balancing the books – but my thoughts returned to Alison and her family. I had acted for her for over ten years, so I was aware of her troubled relationship with her brother.

Shaun had always been the golden boy. Their father had made him the chief executive officer of the family business at the age of thirty, responsible for buying, selling and developing property worth hundreds of millions of dollars.

Although Alison worked two days a week as a yoga teacher, she did this mainly as a hobby; her family's wealth meant she did not need to work. A woman in her mid-fifties, she had divorced her husband after about a year and gone to live on an ashram in India for three years. I didn't mind Alison, but she was a difficult client: very anxious, needy and demanding.

She'd mentioned liquidity problems. What sort of trouble could have beset this long-established property empire?

I arrived early at Shaun Henshaw's Bourke Street office and grabbed a coffee at the café downstairs while I waited for our ten o'clock appointment. As I looked around the opulent foyer with its marble floor and huge Brett Whiteley painting, I wondered whether all this wealth was in jeopardy. If it was, it would be a spectacular fall from grace for one of Melbourne's most respected and affluent families. My phone beeped, alerting me to the appointment, so I took a last mouthful of coffee and rode the lift to the twenty-sixth floor.

'Mr Henshaw is expecting you,' the receptionist said as she led me down the hall to a huge boardroom with plush green carpet, an oak table and a Papunya dot painting on the wall. The floor-to-ceiling windows offered a view of the city's towers and the wall near the door was lined with books on architecture and interior design.

'Mr Henshaw will be with you in a moment,' the receptionist said, indicating a chair facing the window. 'Please, take a seat.'

A few minutes later a tall, distinguished man with grey hair strode through the door. He was dressed in a black suit with a white, open-necked shirt.

'Brendan Baer,' I said as he shook my hand. His blue eyes were intense, and I felt he was sizing me up.

'Pleased to meet you,' he said after a pause. As we sat down opposite each other, his receptionist poured two cups of coffee and placed one in front of each of us.

'I understand you are my sister's accountant,' he said coldly. 'How can I help you?' There was a hint of annoyance in his tone and he fidgeted with his cufflink.

'Yes, that's why I'm here, Mr Henshaw. She's aware of problems in the family business, and as co-director, she has some concerns – especially regarding her own finances.'

There was a long, uncomfortable silence.

I continued. 'I'm sure you're aware that, as a yoga instructor, Alison doesn't earn much money and relies on her monthly income from the family business.'

He continued to look at me coldly, then shrugged and nodded as if to say, *So what do you want me to do about it?*

There followed another awkward silence so I went on. 'Alison asked me to talk to you to find out what has happened.'

Shaun turned towards the bookshelves and seemed deep in thought. When he finally spoke, his tone was measured. 'It's not good,' he said. 'As you would know, the property market has collapsed. The value of our assets has decreased from $800 million to $400 million and our debt remains at $500 million. The banks have frozen all our accounts and unless we reduce our borrowings and correct our lending ratio, the banks will take possession of all our assets.'

I inhaled sharply, shocked by what he had told me. How could Shaun have structured the family's assets in such a risky and irresponsible way? By not planning for a possible collapse in the property market, he had broken one of the fundamental rules of business. But then I remembered Shaun Henshaw had a reputation for being a bit of a cowboy.

'I'm very sorry to hear of your misfortunes,' I said neutrally. 'How are you planning to ride this out?'

Shaun sipped his coffee. After a moment he looked at me and said, 'We are currently talking with a private equity fund. Hopefully, they will buy our asset portfolio rather than leaving us at the mercy of the banks.'

'So, where does that leave Alison?'

He folded his arms across his chest, unable to disguise his hostility. 'Quite frankly, I don't give a shit about Alison. She's never done a day's work in her life. Maybe she should get a real job.'

I looked at him in astonishment, taken aback by the extent of his animosity.

'But you have an obligation to continue those payments—'

'Mr Baer, did you not hear me? I told you the banks have frozen all our assets and I don't have access to any bank accounts.'

I nodded and said, 'I now have a clearer understanding of the situation, Mr Henshaw. Thank you.'

'I'm pleased to hear that, Mr Baer,' he said briskly. Then he stood up, indicating that the meeting was over.

As I walked out of the building I reflected on Shaun's antagonism towards his sister. I wondered at the source of the rancour between them. No doubt there was a story there that still held them in its grip.

Back in my car I rang Alison and told her I had just met Shaun and had some news for her. 'Can I come over?' I asked.

I drove along St Kilda Road, then turned right into Page Street. Double-storey Victorian terraces and rows of tall plane trees lined both sides of the street. Arriving at Alison's house I climbed the polished stone steps and knocked on the door.

'Hello Brendan, come in,' Alison croaked as she opened the door. She was still in her floral dressing-gown. There were bags under her eyes and her hair was limp and greasy.

I followed her down the hall into the study where she motioned me to sit opposite her near the window. 'So Brendan, cut to the chase. Am I going to get some money?'

I paused, considering how to broach the subject. 'Alison, the news is not good. Your brother has over-borrowed and because the value of the assets has fallen significantly, the banks intend to take possession of the family business.'

'So what exactly does that mean? What're the consequences for me?'

'According to Shaun, the bottom line is this: if he can't negotiate his way out of this financial mess, you and the family will end up with nothing.'

Alison looked at me with wide angry eyes. 'That's bullshit!' she exclaimed. 'I don't trust him, not for one minute. He'd have plenty of money stashed away.'

'Be that as it may, Alison, he says he is not able to access any money for you.'

'Well, what am I going to live on?' she shrieked.

'Do you have any money in your personal bank account?'

'Very little.'

'Maybe speak with your parents. See if they're willing to help you.'

'My parents? Oh god, Brendan, I can't believe this is happening.' She ran a hand through her hair. 'I guess I've got no choice.'

'Good luck, Alison. And don't hesitate to call me if I can be of any assistance.'

That night I was having dinner with my wife in the city when my phone rang. I glanced at the caller ID.

'Sorry Sarah,' I said, 'it's a client. I really need to take this call.' I walked outside, away from the noise of rowdy patrons eating and laughing.

'Brendan, hope I haven't got you at a bad time, but I've just spoken to my father and I need to talk to you,' Alison said.

'I'm having dinner with Sarah in the city,' I said. 'How can I help you?'

'Dad said he will give me some immediate financial support but suggested I get Shaun to negotiate with the banks to release a couple of properties we own in the city so I have an ongoing source of income.'

'I doubt that's possible, Alison,' I said, one hand over my ear to block out the city noise. 'I'm sure the banks will want to take possession of all the properties to cover their debt.'

'I know. Dad warned me the banks may not co-operate, but he suggested Shaun try at the very least.'

I hesitated for a moment and said, 'I'm worried that you might be over-reaching Alison, but if you want me to talk to Shaun, I'm happy to do so.'

'Yes. Please speak with him and tell him I want two properties.' She named two buildings, one in Collins Street, the other in Bourke Street. 'And you can also tell him that if I don't get them I will not co-operate. I will not sign the documents with the banks.'

'Is everything okay?' Sarah asked when I resumed my seat.

I took a deep breath and said, 'Remember my client Alison Kavanagh? She's part of the Henshaw family. I think you've met her once or twice. Anyway, she's been living off her family's wealth, but now the empire has come crashing down and the banks are about to seize their assets.'

Sarah frowned. 'So how is she going to live?'

'Well, she's arm-wrestling her brother into securing two city properties for her.'

'Will the banks co-operate?' Sarah asked.

'I doubt it, but Alison wants to try.'

Sarah looked at me sceptically. 'Good luck with that.'

The following Monday I was again sitting in Shaun Henshaw's boardroom peering at his dot painting and his shelves of art books. Shaun sat opposite me, his pale lean face rough with stubble, looking bone weary.

'My client has asked me to tell you that she wants to secure two city properties as part of the settlement with the banks,' I said.

'Does she now?' Shaun snapped, his face twisting with frustration and annoyance. He jumped up from his chair, walked to the window and sat down again.

I tried to maintain my poise, but I felt intimidated by his aggressive demeanour. 'As a director of the company, Alison knows that you require her signature on any agreement you reach with the banks. She has instructed me to inform you that unless she secures the two properties, she won't sign any document.'

'She's bluffing,' Shaun said flatly. 'As a director she has a legal obligation to sign.'

'I wouldn't push her,' I countered.

Shaun looked straight at me and barked, 'Any other demands?'

'No, that's it,' I replied blandly.

'She knows that she's got me over a barrel so she thinks she can blackmail me! She's using and abusing her power as a director.'

'You can interpret it any way you like, Mr Henshaw, but she wants and needs those properties.'

'Well, I have no choice, but I can't make any promises. The banks are very tough negotiators. I'll try, that's all I'm prepared to do,' he said, standing abruptly and walking me to the door.

'Let me know how you get on,' I said over my shoulder.

I knew that Shaun was correct; it was indeed blackmail and I wondered – not for the first time – about Alison's motives. On the face of it, she was driven by need. But I had a sense that deeper forces were at work.

In the afternoon of the following week I was at Alison's place, sitting with her in the study drinking coffee. A cold wind blew through the bare plane trees and I noticed the darkening sky.

'You look troubled,' Alison said. 'What's the matter?'

'I'm not sure that the banks will release the properties, Alison. They have a lot at stake. They need to reclaim as many assets as possible to recoup any losses and reduce the debt to satisfy head office. I think it would be more reasonable for you to ask for one property. It will make Shaun's life easier and he'll be more likely to be able to negotiate a deal.'

'Brendan,' Alison said sharply, 'you need to know that I am not interested in making my brother's life easier.'

Finally, we were at the crux of the matter. Alison clearly hated Shaun and although she needed the money, she was making the most of this financial disaster to exact some sort of revenge.

She gave me a straight look and said, 'Let me tell you a story about my brother. You may not want to hear this, Brendan, but I think I owe it to you to explain why I'm so angry and unforgiving of Shaun. I take no pleasure in wielding my power but it's my chance to finally pay him back in part for his years of abuse when we were teenagers. You see, at night he would come into my bedroom . . .'

As she uncovered those horrific memories I felt my scalp begin to crawl. The blood drained from my face.

'. . . and when I asked my parents to put a lock on the door, they refused.'

I broke into a cold sweat. Alison wiped her eyes with a resolute gesture and said, 'So . . . as far as I'm concerned, fuck him! No properties, no signature.

Sarah was at book club when I got home, and the house felt emptier than usual. I stared vacantly into the night, hearing Alison say *he would come into my bedroom . . .* I tried to calm myself by breathing deeply, but it didn't help. I went into my study and sat at the desk for a while, opened a book and stared blankly at it then closed it. I began to wander aimlessly through the rooms of the house, then strolled out onto the patio and stared across the yard.

The wind had dropped and the sky was clear. It was very cold. I heard a frantic buzzing and went to investigate. A spider had spun a web across the corner of the rail and trapped a beetle. It was struggling desperately to free itself.

I blew hard on the beetle, and the web gave way. The beetle fell to the deck and scurried off.

Next day, I was sitting at my desk with my head in the Tax Act when Jane called me on the intercom. 'It's Shaun Henshaw on line three.'

'Put it through,' I replied, wondering about the purpose of his call.

'Mr Baer, Brendan, I'm ringing to tell you I've just been with the representatives of the banks.'

'How did you go?'

'All good,' he said. His voice cracked and he paused. 'After intense negotiations I've finally come to an arrangement with them. What's more, I even got them to agree to set aside the Collins Street property for Alison.'

I felt myself go cold. Choosing my words carefully, I said, 'I'm not sure that will fly, Shaun. As you know, Alison is adamant – she wants those two properties.'

Shaun was silent for a moment, then he said, 'Do me a favour, Brendan. Speak to her and see if she will agree to one property. Explain to her that it wasn't easy to get the bank to this point – to release one property, let alone two. And I suspect a second will be out of the question.'

'Okay Shaun. I'll pass it on.'

I hung up, looked up Alison's number in my directory and rang her.

'Alison, I've just spoken to your brother.'

'And?'

'He rang to say he has done a deal with the banks.'

'Yes?'

'He said the bank will only release one property and he doesn't think they will budge on the second.'

Alison's reaction was instantaneous. It was as though someone had thrown a match on a pile of straw. 'Forget it. Fuck him! It's two properties or no signature.' Her voice trembled with rage.

There was a long silence. I sat in my chair trying to control my breathing. Not wanting to upset her further, I thought carefully before I spoke. 'So, Alison, do you want me to tell him the deal is off?'

'Absolutely, the deal is off. Two properties or no signature!'

'Leave it with me,' I said as I put down the phone, sighing heavily.

I took a coffee break to collect my thoughts and rehearse what I was going to say to Shaun. Then I picked up the phone and dialled his number. I told him I'd spoken with Alison and that she would not sign any documents unless she secured those two properties.

'What the fuck? She has no understanding of the commercial world whatsoever! Here I am busting my gut for the family, trying to keep the ship afloat, as I have done for the last twenty years, and all she can do is blast holes in it . . .'

'Sorry Shaun, but I tried.'

'You know where this leaves us,' he hissed. 'If I tell the bank she is refusing to sign, they will immediately appoint a liquidator.'

'Maybe go back and try again.'

I heard a click, indicating that Shaun had slammed down the phone.

A fortnight later I rang Alison to let her know I had just received a call from Shaun telling me he had renegotiated the deal with the banks and they were now willing to release the two properties.

'Pleased to hear it,' Alison said mildly. But when I told her she was required to attend the solicitor's office at ten the next morning so that all parties to the transaction could sign the relevant documents she said, 'Brendan, that time is no good for me. It's bad karma, the stars aren't aligned. I will only sign at four o'clock.'

After all we had been through I couldn't believe what I was hearing. 'Alison, this is very complicated. Rescheduling settlement means that bankers from three different banks, with their lawyers, your brother and his lawyer and lawyers for the group will all be inconvenienced.'

'Brendan, I don't care. It's bad karma,' she repeated.

Did she really believe this nonsense, or was she twisting the knife one last time while she still had power over her brother? From the moment Alison knew Shaun was in a vulnerable position, she had exploited every opportunity to humiliate him. Perhaps it was the only chance she had to pay him back for the abuse.

By five that afternoon, all the parties to the agreement had signed the documents and left. Shaun, Alison and I sat on in the boardroom for a few moments.

Shaun walked to the window and looked out over the city. With his back to Alison, he said, 'Couldn't help yourself, could you Alison?'

'What do you mean?' Alison said.

Shaun turned to face her. 'You know exactly what I mean.'

'And you know exactly why,' Alison said coldly.

Shaun stared at her, his hands clenched, his knuckles white. 'You need to get over it and move on.' A crimson flush spread across his face.

Alison turned away from Shaun, and gave me a look full of meaning. 'That's what I'd expect from you. You have no idea of what you've done and the harm you've caused – the trauma, my inability to maintain a relationship, the years of therapy . . .'

'Look, I've been busting my gut trying to do the right thing for the family, and for you—'

'Bullshit. You were trying to do the right thing for *yourself*.'

Shaun stared at Alison, his pupils enormous. He opened his mouth to speak, then stopped. 'Alison, this is not the time or the place—'

'You just don't get it, do you?'

'What do you want from me? What do you want me to say? What's done is done.'

'*Sorry* might be a start.'

Shaun shrugged contemptuously and said, 'Sorry for what? Sorry because I picked on you and made fun of you when you were a kid. Okay . . . sorry. Feel better now?' There was a vacant, dead look in his eyes.

Alison gave a bitter little laugh. 'Actually no. I was wrong. Nothing you say or do will ever make me feel better.' She stood up, and I followed her to the door. 'But thanks for the properties.'

Guinea Gold

'The stock market seems strong,' Nick said. 'I'm always interested in a good opportunity, despite Judy's naysaying . . .'
He dropped the dental probe on the tray.

Matthew lifted his eyebrows and made a suitable sound in his throat. As well as being a longstanding patient, he was Nick's stockbroker.

'Your teeth are looking good,' Nick said, checking them one last time before replacing the tiny mirror. 'I don't need to see you for another twelve months.'

'Great,' Matthew said as he sat up in the chair.

'Rinse if you like.'

Matthew glanced at the tray of scalers, mirrors, probes, and other disturbing instruments, then took a sip from the plastic cup and gargled. He got to his feet and turned to Nick. 'Guinea Gold.'

'What?'

'Guinea Gold. It's a small gold-mining company in Guinea, in West Africa.'

Nick cocked his head. 'And, you're telling me about it because . . .?'

'The company is due to be listed on the stock exchange within months, and when that happens, shareholders will make a fortune. It's a sure thing, Nick.'

Nick smiled behind his mask as he contemplated the possibilities. But then he remembered the extent of his debt and all his other financial obligations.

'Let me know if you're interested,' Matthew said as he put on his jacket.

'I'm interested – it sounds like an amazing opportunity – but the truth is I'm already overcommitted. And Judy is super conservative with money, as you know; she'd kill me if I stretched us too thin.'

'But gold is a reliable investment, Nick. This isn't high risk.'

Nick shrugged. 'With our mortgage and the repayments on the new investment property, I don't have a lot of disposable income.'

'Oh well, it's a shame,' Matthew said as he headed for the door. 'Nice to see you, Nick. I'd better get going. I want to be back at the office before the market closes.'

'I'll see you to the lift,' Nick said as they walked along the hall.

Just before the lift doors closed Matthew said, 'Guinea Gold – if you change your mind, you know where to find me.'

$\wp$

'So, how was your day?' Judy asked. A warm summer breeze blew in through the open window of the dining room.

'I saw Matt today,' Nick said as he finished off his pasta.

Judy looked up at him. There was a long pause before she said, 'And how is he?'

'He's good,' Nick said. 'No work needed. He's excited about a stock called Guinea Gold. Reckons we should buy some.'

Judy put down her fork. 'Nick, you're not really considering it, are you? Matthew is a good patient but remember the last hot tip he gave you.'

'This is different Judy; it's gold,' Nick said. 'Apparently this company is about to float, and when it does, investors will make millions. And besides, some tips are good, others bad; that's the nature of the game. Don't forget, he's also put us onto some good deals.'

Judy started to say something then stopped. She picked up her fork and gazed out the window. After a moment she said firmly, 'We've already extended ourselves by buying that investment property . . .'

Nick didn't look up from his meal, so she continued. 'As it is I feel as though we're in a financial straitjacket. It's too risky.'

Nick sighed. 'Yeah, you're probably right.' He collected his plate and cutlery. 'All done?' he said, taking her plate before she could reply and heading for the kitchen.

On Saturday morning, Nick met Judy's brother David for their regular golf game. Heavy rain clouds hung over the course, so they decided to wait in the clubhouse until the weather cleared.

'How are you going?' David asked.

'To tell you the truth, David, I'm struggling,' Nick replied.

'I'm sorry to hear that. What's up?'

'It's Judy.' Nick sighed.

David said nothing, so Nick went on, 'She's . . . I don't know, she's so controlling.'

David took a deep breath. 'Why do you say that?'

Nick hesitated, then said, 'I've been offered this amazing investment opportunity,' he stopped for a moment to clear his throat, 'but Judy won't even discuss it.'

David looked at him in surprise. 'Why not?'

'She's afraid of the risk. She carries on as if we could lose everything, that it could all come crashing down around us.'

David shook his head slowly. 'But Nick, this is not new; you know this about Judy; it's how we were brought up.'

'But how come you're not like that?' Nick said. 'You never seem to be that anxious about money.'

'I am, Nick, but not to the same degree. I've run my own business for years and that's helped me manage some of my anxiety,' David said.

'I know your parents lost everything during the war, but this is different. I'm talking about an investment opportunity. There are no Nazis, no paratroopers, no Poles raiding Jewish homes . . .'

'I know, but Nick, we still bear the scars. When you've been constantly reminded of the transience of things as a child, you carry it with you for the rest of your life.'

'I guess so, and you're right, none of this is new, but it's really beginning to grind me down,' Nick said. 'To be honest, sometimes I feel like I'm suffocating . . .'

'Come on,' David said, 'let's get outside and practise our putting at least.'

Nick glanced up at the sky and followed David out to the putting green.

'You know,' David said, 'when we were kids Judy saved all her pocket money, and if anyone gave her lollies, she hid them under her bed.'

'Why am I not surprised,' Nick said flatly.

'Enough already,' David said, shoving his putter back in his bag. 'The sky's clearing, let's play some golf instead.'

The following morning Nick opened the blinds and noticed that the rain from the previous day had cleared and sunlight was glittering on the leaves. Turning towards Judy he said, 'It looks beautiful out there. Let's go out for breakfast.'

There was a long silence.

'I've been cooped up in the surgery all week,' Nick continued. 'I need to get out.'

'Not true. You played golf with David yesterday,' Judy said as she sat up in bed.

'Yes, but all week I've been stuck in the surgery with my hands down people's throats. And anyway, I love going out for breakfast.'

'Nick, I've got eggs in the fridge. And I can make us coffee . . .'

'Oh, c'mon Judy. Let's live a little. We can afford breakfast out now and then,' Nick said, his jaw tightening.

'I just don't see the point of paying good money for eggs and coffee, when we've got plenty right here,' Judy said. 'It's a waste of money.'

Nick took a deep breath. 'Judy, I need to get out. I'll go without you if I have to.'

'Do what you like, Nick. I'm happy to stay home,' Judy said as he walked towards the bathroom.

Nick drove to his favourite café in Brunswick. He chose a seat at the communal table and immediately felt his shoulders relax. A Rod Stewart song was playing and a man sitting opposite was tucking into his avocado and salmon with relish. A toddler with chocolate smeared all over her face scooped up her babycino while her parents looked on dotingly. Seeing couples holding hands, enjoying their leisure time, Nick wished he was married to someone who took pleasure in the same things he did.

Judy was reading by the window in the lounge when Nick walked in.

'What are you reading?' he asked, in an attempt at reconciliation.

'David Malouf,' Judy muttered, not taking her eyes from the page.

'Judy, can you please put down the book. There's something I want to talk to you about.'

She looked up at him.

'I was thinking about Guinea Gold while I was having breakfast.'

Judy looked back at her book, her mouth tight.

'I know what you think,' Nick continued, 'but it could be a financial windfall.'

Judy rolled her eyes.

'If we don't do it, we'll regret it.'

'If you do it and it goes pear-shaped, we'll regret it. And I will never forgive you – you know I hate the stock market,' she said.

Nick felt his shoulders stiffen and he opened his mouth to speak, but Judy hadn't finished. 'Every time Matthew puts us onto a stock I'm anxious for weeks.'

'Yes, but we make money!'

'The last time we lost money,' Judy snapped.

Nick sighed.

'To me, the stock market is like playing roulette at the casino; it's no different to gambling,' she said.

Nick realised that a chasm had opened up between him and Judy and nothing he said would convince her of the merits of this deal. He got up and walked to the window. Outside, trees shifted in the breeze, their branches casting a shadow over the lawn. He felt suddenly lonely.

'Look at the Goldblums,' Judy went on, 'they lost their life savings because their broker had a so-called hot tip.'

'It's impossible to talk to you,' Nick said, 'I'm wasting my time. You can only reason with reasonable people,' he said as he walked out of the room.

$\wp$

Three weeks later Nick's phone rang while he was driving to work. The caller ID showed it was Matthew. He pulled into the first parking space and answered.

'To what do I owe the pleasure?' Nick said. 'I hope it's not toothache.'

'No,' Matthew laughed. 'I just wanted to update you on Guinea Gold.'

Nick was silent for a moment. 'Oh. Look, I discussed it with Judy and she is dead-set against it. She can't cope with any degree of uncertainty or financial risk. She's really wary of putting money into the stock market.'

'That's a very limited view,' Matthew said. 'After all, people have been investing in the market for decades and many of them have made a lot of money.'

'You don't have to convince me, my friend,' Nick said with a sigh.

'Clearly Judy just doesn't understand. This is gold; the risk is minimal.'

'I know, but talking to Judy about the stock market is like banging my head against a brick wall.'

'Nick, the company is going to float in about six months and when it does the price–earnings ratio is expected to go through the roof.'

Nick felt blood rush to his cheeks. 'Don't . . .' he groaned.

'Look, can I speak candidly here?' Matthew said. 'I think you need to stop listening to your wife. Her crazy hang-up about the stock market has no basis in reality. I think you need to make a unilateral decision here, Nick, because if these shares float, which they will, and go gangbusters, which they will, and you haven't invested, you will kick yourself.'

'I appreciate your honesty, Matt, and you're probably right.'

'There's an initial capital raising to increase the size of the business. If you want, I can get you into it. If you put in a hundred thousand dollars, on current estimates you could make in excess of a million.'

'Let me think about it,' Nick said and put down the phone.

Driving along St Kilda Road towards the surgery, he fantasised about what he would do with the money. He had wanted a new car for years and he and Judy hadn't been overseas since their honeymoon. But then he recalled the last time he'd wanted to buy a new car. Judy had muttered, 'What's wrong with the one you've got?' And with a sinking heart, he remembered her protests when he'd canvassed the idea of an overseas trip: 'It's so expensive, Nick. Let's just go to Sydney instead. The beaches are nicer there anyway.'

Nick thought – as he often did – about the life he'd lived before he married. He scrolled through his memories of the many dinners he'd eaten out with friends, the jazz bars they'd frequented, their carefree weekends away . . . It had all come to an end. He sighed. Did he miss it? It was not in his nature to cultivate regrets; nevertheless, he now began to consider the many things in his life that frustrated him, especially Judy's attitude to money. Had he made a mistake in marrying her? He had been so mad about her back then.

ꝑ

The following morning Nick arrived at the surgery early and rang Matthew before his first patient. 'I won't keep you long, Matt,' he said, 'but can you tell me more about the Guinea Gold deal?'

'Nick, I wasn't expecting to hear from you. Have you changed your mind?'

'I've given it a lot of thought and I trust your judgement on this.'

'Good man,' Matthew said warmly.

'And to be honest, I'm really over Judy holding me back. If I don't take up your offer and Guinea Gold floats successfully, I'll be seriously pissed off.'

'Nick, this stock is really hot; people are clamouring to get in on the deal, so we'll need to act quickly. I'll get you as much as I can. What's your upper limit?'

'If the stocks are as good as you say, I'll spend up to two hundred thousand,' Nick said. A nurse stuck her head around the door to say his patient had arrived but he waved her away. 'Look, I've got to go, but get me in on this, Matt, please.'

Nick ended the call, removed his glasses, and rubbed his eyes. He moved his head from side to side, releasing the tension in his neck. He felt a sudden sense of lightness and independence, and when he went to meet his patient, he had a spring in his step.

He arrived home that evening to find Judy in the den watching *MasterChef*. She looked up at him. 'Oh, you look cheerful.'

'Yeah,' Nick said with a shrug, 'had a good day. Judy, it's freezing in here. Why isn't the heating on?'

'Well, this blanket is keeping me warm,' she said, eyes back on the television.

'Suit yourself, but I'm not sitting in the cold,' he said as he turned on the heater.

A few months later, Nick was writing up some medical notes when Matthew rang.

'Nick, my friend, welcome to your new life: you're a multi-millionaire!'

'What?' Nick said, dropping his pen. 'What on earth are you talking about?'

'Guinea Gold floated this morning,' Matthew exclaimed.

'And . . .'

'And they reckon the stock price will continue to go north tomorrow and the next day. Mate, you could end up with about three million dollars.'

Nick felt his heart leap and adrenalin wash through his bloodstream. 'Oh my god, I don't know what to say . . .' he stammered. 'Thank you. Thank you so much, Matt.'

'Just doing my job,' Matthew said. 'Enjoy!'

Nick abandoned his notes – he couldn't concentrate and he didn't want to make an error. Instead he phoned his accountant to share the news.

'Brendan? Nick Drummond. How are things?'

'Fine. How can I help you, Nick?'

'I'm going to have a tax problem this year, mate. I invested in Guinea Gold and the company floated this morning.'

'Congratulations, so how big will the problem be precisely?'

'Around three million dollars on top of the usual.'

Brendan whistled softly. 'That's quite a problem. Let me think about it and I'll get back to you. In the meantime, where are you celebrating?'

'No plans yet. I'll see what Judy wants to do.'

'Well, have one for me,' said Brendan and rang off.

As Nick drove home, his mind turned to Judy. Would she share in his joy and celebrate this windfall with him? He hoped so. He allowed himself to picture the red Audi he had always wanted, the European countries on his bucket list and the beach house in a pocket of the Mornington Peninsula he'd had his eye on.

But what if Judy threw the proverbial wet blanket over it all, as she always did? He swallowed hard. What should he do? Should he leave her?

'Come out onto the porch,' he said to Judy as he closed the fridge door. She was at the sink peeling potatoes.

'I'm busy with dinner right now, Nick. Can it wait?' she said, not looking up.

'No, it can't,' Nick said firmly. 'There's something I need to tell you.'

Judy sighed, wiping her hands on her apron, and followed her husband to the porch.

'Judy, contrary to your advice, I invested in Guinea Gold—'

'Nick!' she said, twisting the apron in her hands.

'Please, let me finish Judy. The stock floated this morning and we have made a lot, and I mean *a lot*, of money.'

His wife was silent. For a long moment she stood very still. 'Well, that's a relief,' she said finally.

'But I need to tell you, Judy, that instead of squirrelling away the money at a low interest rate, I intend to spend it. '

She gaped at him as he strode into the house and came back with a bottle of Krug and two flutes.

'Hold these,' he said. 'Tomorrow I'm going to buy that Audi I've always wanted. And I'd like us to take a nine-month sabbatical in Europe.' He busied himself with the wire muselet and waited for her to say something, but she seemed utterly lost for words.

'I really want you to come with me, Judy,' he said, turning her to face him. 'It's been too long since we had fun together.' He began to ease the cork from the bottle. 'But you need to know that, even if you decide not to, I will go, regardless.'

The cork shot across the garden and champagne surged from the bottle.

'Don't waste it!' Judy cried. She held out a glass. 'I love champagne. I don't know why we don't have it more often.' Then she threw back her head and laughed.

Divorce

'I'd better take this,' I said to my wife. 'Do you mind? It's a client.'

Sarah sighed, shrugged, and went on eating her dinner.

'Hi Brendan, it's Erica. I'm sorry to disturb you.'

'No worries, Erica. How are you?'

'Actually . . . not good.' I heard her sigh.

'Oh? I'm sorry to hear that. What's wrong?'

'Do you have time to talk?'

It was unusual for a client to ring me at home on a Friday night, but Erica and Ross were good friends as well as clients. As I got up from the table and went into the study, I wondered whether Ross had had another health scare, or perhaps they were having trouble with their kids.

'Please go on, Erica,' I said. 'I'm alone now.'

She hesitated. 'Brendan, you know Ross and I have . . . been having difficulties for some time . . .'

'Yes, but I thought you were having counselling?'

'We've been seeing a psychologist for some months now, but we're getting nowhere. To tell you the truth, Brendan, my heart's just not in this marriage anymore. I've decided to throw in the towel,' she said.

'Wow!' I said, taking a deep breath. 'That's a big step, Erica.' I took off my glasses and rubbed my temple. Despite all the compromises and flare-ups in their relationship, I had always assumed Erica and Ross would slug it out and that their marriage would survive. I'd known them since university days, and I realised I had a stake in their staying together – if only for old time's sake.

'I'm really sorry to hear it's come to this, Erica. But why the sudden change?'

'Brendan, you know as well as anyone that I haven't been happy for some time; Ross hasn't exactly been a faithful husband. Yet I stayed with him for the sake of the boys and keeping the family together. But I've had enough. It's time for me to look after myself.'

I cleared my throat and said, 'Have you told the boys?'

'Yes. They weren't surprised, but they're very upset, not surprisingly.'

I was still gobsmacked by Erica's decision to separate. I'd always assumed that Ross would be the one to leave, given his philandering.

'Look, the reason I'm ringing you, Brendan, is because Ross and I want to try to avoid getting bogged down with lawyers. Can you maybe come over and help us divide the family assets? You've been our accountant for over twenty years and we both trust you implicitly.'

'Of course, Erica. When suits?'

'How's tomorrow night at eight?'

'Perfect.'

$$\wp$$

'That was Erica,' I said to Sarah as I went back into the kitchen. 'Guess what?'

'Don't tell me. She's leaving him?' Sarah said, closing the dishwasher. 'That's been a long time coming.'

'Really? I thought they'd stick it out till the bitter end. Anyway, they want me to help them divide the assets; they're hoping to avoid lawyers . . .'

Sarah snorted. 'Good luck with that,' she said, giving me a sceptical look.

'Yeah . . . well, anyway, I'll do my best. But all those years of Ross's screwing around must have eroded any trust between them. And as you know, they're both completely obsessed with money. It's going to get ugly, you can be sure of that. They're kidding themselves if they think this won't end up in court.'

The following evening, I climbed the wide stone stairs to the door of Erica and Ross's Toorak home. As I reached for the bell I heard raised voices. But once I'd announced myself, the argument seemed to die down. Through the stained-glass panels that flanked the door I saw Erica approaching.

'Hi Brendan,' she said huskily. Her face was pale and her eyes looked bloodshot, as if she'd been crying. 'I really appreciate you coming over. It's turning into a bloody nightmare.'

'I hope I can help,' I said.

Ross threw me a glance as I followed Erica into the kitchen. His face was flushed. 'Thanks for coming, Brendan. I hope we can sort this out amicably.' He turned away and gazed out the window at the gum trees that towered over the back garden and I heard him mutter under his breath, 'But I have my doubts.'

'Sit down, Brendan,' Erica said. She was biting her bottom lip to keep herself from crying.

As I pulled out a chair I looked at Ross and said, 'I went through your file, so, shall we get started?'

He nodded, and Erica indicated that I should continue.

'Right, well, according to our records, your family assets consist of this house, which is worth about five million dollars, the trusts have two investment properties worth about two million dollars each, and the share portfolio is worth three million.'

Erica picked at her nails. Ross looked queasy, as though he were about to be fleeced of all his money.

'I think the best way to proceed is for each of you to be in a separate room so you can talk to me privately. Erica, will you stay in the kitchen? And Ross, can you please go into the study. I'll come and talk to you first.'

I followed Ross out of the kitchen and walked along the hall, admiring the two Boyds as I passed.

Once in the study, I closed the door. Ross was seated at the heavy mahogany desk and I took a seat in the chair opposite.

'I'm sorry to hear about this, Ross. How are you holding up?'

'To tell you the truth, I'm shocked,' he said, looking stricken. 'I never thought it would come to this.' He paused, shaking his head dolefully. 'Look, I know I haven't been an angel, but for the last ten years I promise you I've been faithful! I've looked after Erica and the boys . . . I can't believe she's actually going through with this. I'm gutted.'

'Yeah, I was really surprised when I got the call. I thought you guys had come to terms with some of your differences . . .'

'Yes, well, Erica has always been unpredictable. Anyway, Brendan, let's get down to business.'

'Of course. So how do you want to divide up the assets?' I asked.

He looked at me squarely. 'I think it should be fifty-fifty.'

I nodded. 'Let me speak with Erica and see what she says.' I got up and went to the kitchen. I doubted she would accept it; assets are usually divided in favour of the wife, who is often compensated for not having an ongoing source of income due to family obligations.

Nevertheless, I had to convey Ross's wishes; I was merely the messenger.

'Erica,' I said, 'Ross would like to divide the assets equally.' I sat down. She looked at me and blinked nervously. After a long moment she stood up, put her hands on her hips and said, 'No way. I want a sixty–forty split. After all I've been through with him and his string of affairs . . .'

Yep, I thought to myself, I saw this coming a mile off.

'I'll see what I can do,' I said, keeping my tone neutral.

Once in the study I conveyed Erica's wishes to Ross. 'She says your extramarital affairs have caused her a lot of pain and embarrassment.'

Ross looked at me but didn't seem to be seeing me at all. 'That's bullshit,' he snapped.

Caught between these two fractious parties I was beginning to feel uneasy. 'Listen,' I said, motioning him to calm down, 'we need to talk about it.'

'What's there to talk about?' he retorted.

'Well, from Erica's point of view—'

'Firstly, I haven't been with another woman in ten years so I don't know what she's on about!'

'Yes, but what about the first twenty years of your marriage?'

Ross cut me off. 'She's never done a day's work in her life! I've been on call at the hospital, day and night, seven days a week for thirty years. If it wasn't for me, we'd have nothing!'

I nodded briskly. 'Let me see what I can do,' I said as I left the room.

I knew that a court would award Erica more than fifty per cent, and wondered if I could convince them to agree to this settlement.

As I entered the kitchen I noticed Erica had taken down a bottle of brandy and poured herself a shot. She offered me a glass but, as much as I wanted one, I declined.

'Erica,' I began again, 'would you be prepared to compromise on a fifty-five–forty-five per cent split?'

'Has Ross agreed to it?'

'No, but if I convince him, would you be happy?'

She looked at me for a moment, her eyes narrowed. 'No, but I'd accept it,' she said finally. 'I just want this to be over.'

'Okay, good. Let me talk with Ross,' I said.

Back in the study I said, 'Ross, if I can convince Erica to accept fifty-five per cent, would you accept the compromise?'

His eyes widened but he didn't interrupt. Finally, he said, 'What choice do I have, Brendan?'

'I think it's a good decision. Come on, let's go back into the kitchen.'

Ross and I sat down at the kitchen table. 'We've come to an agreement,' I said. Erica was quiet for a moment and looked at me in surprise. Then she smiled and said, 'I'm happy to hear that.'

'Think it over, both of you, and let me know if you want me to ring a lawyer on Monday morning to draft an agreement,' I said.

Gazing out the window Ross murmured, 'Yep, will do.'

'I'll give it some thought,' Erica said, looking drained.

The next morning was overcast and misty, and I could barely make out the people on the far footpath as I walked along Toorak Road to the Manhattan Deli for breakfast. Suddenly, I noticed Ross walking in my direction.

'Brendan, thank you for last night,' he said as he shook my hand.

'No problem. I'd like to say it was a pleasure. But I was happy to help and very pleased you came to an agreement.'

'You know it was a waste of time, Brendan, don't you?' Ross said.

'What? Why do you say that?' I was taken aback.

He looked at me. 'Brendan, after thirty years of marriage I know my wife. Last night was a farce. It was a try-on to see what she could get out of me. She'll want her day in court,' he said bitterly.

'So why did you agree to take part?' I said.

He paused for a moment, then smiled ruefully. 'I was curious to see where this might take us; I wanted to gauge her expectations,' he said. Then he turned to go.

I was sitting at my desk the following Monday morning when my secretary buzzed to say that Erica was at reception, unannounced.

'Please send her in,' I said, turning my attention from the ledgers.

'Hi, Brendan, I was just passing and I thought I'd drop in quickly and bring you up to date.'

I motioned her to take a seat. 'Why, what's the problem?'

'I'm having second thoughts about our agreement,' Erica said as she settled into the chair opposite me. 'I'm not sure whether it's fair. I might be able to do better,' she said. Her mood was bold, confident, very unlike the anxious person I'd encountered at their home.

Inwardly I sighed, thinking that she was quite deluded. 'Erica, even if this goes to court, I doubt you'll do any better,' I said, looking at her intently.

'Maybe, Brendan. But all my friends keep telling me he's a real bastard and I should take him to court.'

I shrugged. 'Look, you've got to do what works for you,' I said. 'But just remember, these things can get very expensive, and even if you are successful, the legal costs may outweigh the benefits.'

She frowned. 'I hear what you say, Brendan, but I want a public hearing. Let everyone know what the devious creep has been up to these past thirty years,' she said as she stood to leave.

When she reached the door, she turned and looked at me with a steely expression. 'You know, Brendan, I've been swallowing my rage for years. I want him to see my teeth.'

Hell hath no fury like a woman scorned, I thought to myself as she closed the door behind her.

℘

Over the next eighteen months I sent trust deeds, financial statements and other documents to each of their lawyers. On the odd occasion Ross would ring to express his frustration with the slow legal process and Erica periodically complained to me about Ross and his lawyers. I had tried to warn them about all of this, but they were hell-bent on seeing this to the bitter end.

One morning I received a phone call from Ross.

'How are you getting on?' I asked.

'Are you free for a coffee?'

'Yes, later today I'm okay.'

'Let's meet at four-thirty at Ned's Bakery in Toorak Road.'

℘

Ross looked thin and worn when he walked into the café. He glanced at me as he sat down and tried to smile, but there was no warmth or joy in his expression.

'What's up?' I asked.

He stared down at his coffee, his eyes narrowing with anger. 'She's impossible,' he said. 'The costs are getting out of hand. So far I've spent $120,000. She's probably spent a similar amount and there's no end in sight.'

'Have you received a court date?'

'Yes,' he said, leaning forward, resting his forearms on the table. 'It's in three weeks.'

'Any chance this could settle out of court?' I said.

'My lawyer says he's going to try to settle on the steps of the court before we go inside.'

'Great. If he could achieve that it would save both of you a lot of money.'

Ross glanced at me, then lowered his eyes. 'If you could come to court that day, Brendan, I'd really appreciate it. You might be able to convince Erica to finally end this tawdry business and avoid bankrupting us both.'

'Of course, just let me know when it is. I'll speak with Erica to get her permission.'

Monday, the day of the court case, was a cold winter's day. Stepping between the puddles, I mounted the steps of the court and looked up at the imposing sandstone building. Ross and his lawyer were in a private meeting room and Erica and her lawyer were standing at the entrance to the court when I arrived.

'As expected, Ross wants a fifty-fifty split,' I heard Erica's lawyer say to her as I approached.

Erica shook her head and said, 'But I want sixty–forty.'

'I suggest you compromise at forty-five–fifty-five,' her lawyer said. 'If this case goes to court the legal costs for a four-day trial could be as high as $15,000 to $18,000 per day. And the emotional trauma of airing dirty linen will be very difficult for both of you.'

Catching Erica's eye, I interjected, 'Erica, if you've got anything to hide, you can be sure it will come out and be used against you.'

She blinked, as if suddenly jolted into a new awareness. She was silent for a long time, glancing around nervously. Then she took a deep breath and said through gritted teeth, 'Okay, okay, just settle it.'

'I'll do what I can,' the lawyer replied as he walked back into the meeting room.

Half an hour later he returned. 'They've finally agreed. It's forty-five–fifty-five,' he said.

Erica took a deep breath. I imagined that she'd be relieved to have come to a settlement, but disappointed with the result.

'You must be pleased it's all over, Erica,' I said. 'I'm really glad you avoided the angst of a court case.'

'Yes, thank god it's over,' she said hoarsely. She looked broken.

Noticing Ross walk out of the meeting room, I excused myself and approached him. 'Congratulations,' I said as I shook his hand.

He wiped his brow with the back of his hand, looking relieved and exhausted. 'Thanks for being here,' he said with a sigh. 'What an epic it turned out to be.'

'To be honest, I didn't do much. I'm just glad you guys managed to sort it out.'

As I turned and walked towards William Street, a flock of birds soared high in the sky and the sun cut through the clouds.

Once in my office I picked up Ross and Erica's file and perched my glasses on the bridge of my nose. Flipping through the pages, I quickly confirmed that the court settlement was exactly the same as the original agreement I had drawn up eighteen months earlier.

I lifted my head and stared out of the window. Erica's bitterness had been simmering beneath the surface for years. I thought about the $250,000 they had incurred in legal costs. And I remembered Ross saying bitterly, 'I know my wife. She'll want her day in court.'

I closed the file.

❦

Daniel Tran: Solicitor

Daniel Tran put down the phone. It was ten o'clock on Thursday morning and he knew he had three options: he could disappear, he could go to jail or he could kill himself.

🕊

'Promise me you'll study hard,' Daniel's father, Anh Tran, had said. 'You must go to university and make something of yourself.' There was a frantic edge to his voice.

Daniel, who was nine at the time, saw how his father's eyes burned and could think of nothing to say. He looked down at the Superman comic he was reading, unable to hold his father's gaze.

'Look at me when I'm talking to you!' Anh shouted. 'And answer me.'

'Yes Dad, I promise,' Daniel mumbled.

'Good. I don't want you to end up living in a housing commission flat doing lowly work like me and your mother,' Anh said as he turned and left the room.

It was late. Anh had finally returned to their small flat, exhausted from cleaning houses, his hands red and peeling. In Vietnam, Anh used to set out for work each day dressed impeccably in a suit and tie. He'd been an engineer at a large manufacturing company – a job he loved and excelled at. But choosing to come to Australia as a refugee in 1977 had changed everything. With very little English and no money, Anh had no choice but to look for menial work.

Even at nine, it was clear to Daniel that although his family had escaped war-torn Vietnam, the loss of his father's profession and status had almost destroyed him.

In his first year at university, Daniel was in the library studying for his exams when he noticed a girl with brown eyes, a round friendly face and short black hair. She often sat in the carrel opposite. Catching her eye one day he said, 'Hi, what are you studying?'

'Biochemistry,' she said with a smile. 'And you?'

'Contract law.'

'Why law?'

'You need to know the law to get around the law,' Daniel quipped.

The girl smiled and raised an eyebrow quizzically.

'I'm joking,' he said. 'The truth is, my parents always wanted me to be a lawyer and I thought it was a good grounding for the business world. I'm Daniel by the way.'

'Hi Daniel. I'm Lily.'

The first time Daniel took Lily out was a warm Sunday night in late October. They caught the tram down to St Kilda Beach and walked to the water's edge, the city skyline shimmering in the distance. Lily talked about her parents, who'd also come to Australia by boat from Vietnam.

'They fled the war,' Lily said, 'like your parents I assume.'

Daniel nodded. 'Our parents wanted us to have a better life, whatever it cost them.'

'Yes. They made sacrifices for us,' Lily said. 'Australians don't understand . . .'

'No, but I'm going to make it up to them. I'm going to make them proud,' Daniel said firmly. 'One day I'll be a respected lawyer, I'll have a big house, and drive a BMW . . .'

Lily laughed. 'I'm sure you will,' she said after a moment. The way Daniel's eyes had narrowed and hardened made her momentarily uneasy, but she admired his determination.

Months after they'd graduated, Daniel and Lily married in a brief ceremony attended by immediate family and close friends. After the dancing, Anh Tran took the microphone.

'My friends and family,' he said. 'You all know how proud I am of Daniel.' There was laughter, but none of it unkind. 'It has not been easy for him.' Anh's voice trembled and he had to stop from time to time to compose himself. 'But he studied hard at university, and even though he had to work part-time to support himself, he graduated with honours.'

At the end of Anh's speech, Lily turned to Daniel and smiled, her eyes wet. Daniel's mother beamed with pride as all the guests stood and applauded.

'I love you Mrs Tran,' Daniel said to Lily once all the guests had gone. 'I promise you that you'll never want for anything; we'll live in a big mansion in Toorak, we'll take holidays overseas and our kids will go to private schools. We'll have a very different life to that of our parents.'

*

Later that same year, Daniel scraped together enough money to put a deposit on a lucrative commercial legal practice. He bought it on vendor terms and arranged to repay the balance out of profits from the practice over three years. Its wealthy clients were successful professionals, property developers and businessmen with large property holdings, the titles of which were held in his vault for safekeeping.

Late one night Lily noticed that Daniel was still awake, lying in bed staring up at the ceiling.

'What is it?' she said quietly. 'What's bothering you?'

'Nothing,' he muttered.

'Why don't you tell me, Daniel? You can confide in me . . .'

'Oh, it's only business worries, Lily. I don't want to bother you.'

'Honey, you've been working such long hours. You're out of the house at seven and sometimes you don't get home till nine. Why don't we take a holiday?'

'I'd love to, believe me, but I can't at the moment. I'm too busy.'

'You promised to take me to Europe for our honeymoon . . .' Lily murmured.

'Yes, I know. But I'm trying to build a business and take care of our families. Give me some time, please.'

Daniel rolled over and closed his eyes but his mind was restless. Despite all his hard work he didn't seem to be as successful as other solicitors. And because of this, he feared the legal community didn't take him seriously: he was still known as 'the boat person', looked down on and patronised. He flung himself onto his back as he remembered a conversation that morning with John Kain, a legal acquaintance.

'Will I see you at the Law Institute's Winter Ball tomorrow night?' John had asked.

Embarrassed at not having received an invitation, Daniel didn't reply. Then he said quietly, 'No, we can't make it unfortunately; prior engagement.'

'Shame to miss it,' John said breezily, and Daniel sensed his disdain. There was no denying it: Daniel Tran was still a battler.

𝄇

One September day, Michael Gray, a property adviser and Daniel's close friend since university, came to see him to discuss a proposal.

Michael took out a cigarette, lit it, then blew smoke from his nostrils. He looked intently at Daniel and said, 'It's a certainty. This property will be rezoned within weeks and you'll triple your money.'

Daniel stood up, walked to the window and stared out at the street. He closed his eyes and rested his forehead against the glass in a gesture of weariness and resignation. Turning back to his friend he said, 'I don't have the money, Michael.'

'It's a shame,' Michael replied. 'You could have made a lot of money in a short period . . .'

Daniel turned and started pacing around his office, then stopped and said, 'Okay, what's the timeframe?'

'Three months at most,' Michael said.

Daniel hesitated. He was just so tired, *bone* tired. For too long now, he'd felt as if he were treading water, working hard but getting nowhere. This deal might give him the windfall that had so far eluded him.

'How soon do you need the money?' he asked.

'In ten days,' Michael said, exhaling another stream of smoke towards the ceiling.

'Okay, give me twenty-four hours to think about it,' Daniel said, and walked Michael to the door.

Back at his desk, he closed all his files and considered the options. He desperately wanted in on this deal – it was the break he needed. But where on earth would he get the money?

Of course he was aware of solicitors defrauding their clients – taking money from trust accounts in order to finance their own business transactions. But the consequences were devastating; he couldn't possibly consider such an option.

What if he made sure he repaid the money within three months? Then it wasn't really stealing; it was more of a loan. He wouldn't be hurting anyone and no one would be the wiser. If all went well, he would earn more in this one transaction than he could in a year of unremitting legal work.

He reopened his files, but as he tried to bend his mind to the legal case, he couldn't stop thinking about Michael's offer. It had sunk its hooks into him.

Daniel came home from work early that evening. Walking through the kitchen, he brushed past Lily with a brief greeting and went straight into the living room. Sunlight streamed through the large glass doors and Daniel started to sweat. A hot, gusty wind blew across the lawn, stirring the dried leaves.

Sitting in his armchair facing the garden, he replayed the conversation with Michael over and over in his head. He started to get to his feet, seemed to remember something, and sat down again heavily.

Lily, who had followed Daniel into the living room, stood just inside the door and observed her husband's tense face. 'What's the problem?' she asked.

Daniel looked up, startled. 'Oh, nothing,' he said. 'Just tired.'

'What can I get you?'

'I'm okay, Lily. Nothing for the moment. Thank you.'

Lost in thought, he fidgeted distractedly with his cufflinks. A voice echoed inside his head: 'Lawyers must be trustworthy.' But the words sounded lame to him. Instead, he calculated the profit he would make if he invested in Michael's venture. He asked himself what could go wrong. Michael had never led anyone astray in the past. He had an excellent reputation as a property developer and his affluence was a testament to his business acumen. The more he thought about it the more Daniel became convinced of the merits of the scheme.

He stood up, took the phone from his pocket and rang Michael. 'I'm in,' he said.

Daniel was sitting at his desk, elbow deep in files, when Michael rang.

'Great news! The rezoning has gone through and we've sold the property.'

'Fantastic,' Daniel said, breathing a sigh of relief. 'When is settlement?' As he exhaled, he realised how uptight he had been over the past three months as he waited anxiously for Michael's news.

'You'll get back all your money and much more in sixty days,' Michael said.

'Oh god, thank you Michael,' he said and put down the phone.

Daniel stood up, but his knees felt weak and his head was spinning. Had he really managed to get away with it? He went over to the liquor cabinet, poured himself a scotch and turned towards the window. It was a warm summer's day and a flock of birds turned in the air outside. Gazing at the skyline, he allowed himself to think about what he would do with the money.

He rang Lily. 'Guess what?' he said, a smile in his voice.

'I can't guess right now, Daniel. I'm at work.'

'Lily, we're finally going on our honeymoon!'

'What?'

'I've just made a lot of money from a property deal. We can go to Europe as we planned.'

'Really? Oh, that's wonderful. I'm so proud of you, honey. I knew you'd do it!'

As he hung up, Daniel smiled to himself. All the stress of worrying about this deal had been worth it. He couldn't wait to tell his father. And he'd better call Brendan, his accountant, about the tax implications.

P

One evening a few weeks later, Daniel was in his study at home writing a memorandum of advice for a client when Michael rang.

'Daniel, I have another property deal if you're interested.'

Daniel sat up straight. If this project was half as lucrative as the first one Michael had put him onto, it was too good to miss.

'How much is it and when do you need the money?'

'It's a high-rise residential development. I'll need fifteen million by the end of the month.'

'That's a lot of money,' Daniel said, his mouth suddenly dry.

'Yes, I know. If the deal is too big, no problem; you don't have to do it.'

Daniel thought about the miserable flat his parents still lived in and his desire to improve their lives.

'I'll find the money,' Daniel said. 'I want in.'

The following morning Daniel went to his vault, selected a bundle of titles to properties owned by clients and, forging their signatures, took them to the bank to borrow against them. By the end of the month Daniel had obtained the fifteen million and passed it on to Michael.

Eighteen months later, Michael rang to say that all the units had been sold and Daniel would receive his original investment of fifteen million dollars plus an additional five million dollars in profits within three months.

He decided to leave work early and visit his parents. As he sat in their cramped living room, he noticed the faded orange curtains and threadbare carpet with the familiar coffee stain near the doorway.

'Dad, I've got good news,' Daniel said. 'I've just completed a successful property deal and I'm going to buy you and Mum a house.'

Anh looked at him in shock. 'Are you sure?'

'Dad, I'm sure. I wouldn't do it if I couldn't afford it. After all you've done for me, it's the least I can do. It's my pleasure.'

'Daniel, that's very generous of you!' Anh said as he stood to embrace his son. 'You've made me very proud.'

As he drove home, Daniel contemplated what he would do with the balance of the proceeds from the sale of the development. He rang Brendan and gave him a heads up about the windfall, then called Michael and arranged to meet him for coffee.

'I've decided to reinvest the proceeds from that deal you put me onto,' Daniel said as they sat opposite each other in their local café. He leaned forward and said, 'Michael, do you have another opportunity?'

'Hang on, Daniel, are you sure you can afford to do that?' Michael said, placing his coffee cup on the saucer. 'Don't you need to repay the money you borrowed from the previous investment?'

Daniel shrugged nonchalantly. 'Rather than repay the fifteen million on the existing loans, I've decided I can just pay interest on them.'

'Isn't that a bit risky?' Michael said, frowning. 'I hope you're not stretching yourself too thin.'

'Michael, you said yourself that the property market is buoyant at the moment and I want to capitalise on it,' Daniel said as he broke off a piece of his croissant.

'Okay mate, it's your decision of course. I've got something coming up that I think you'll be interested in. I'll be in touch.

One Thursday morning a few years later, Daniel received a phone call from Paul Ross, a Melbourne solicitor.

'A month ago,' Paul said to him, 'your client Simon Webb borrowed money on first mortgage from my client Clinton Day.'

'Oh yes, I remember,' Daniel said. 'How can I help you?' He felt a tightening in his jaw and took a deep breath to steady himself.

'Well, it's weird. Clinton didn't receive his interest payment this month and he's wondering why . . .'

Daniel's face started to burn as he recalled interest was due monthly, not quarterly, and he'd forgotten to pay it.

'I tried to ring you on Friday,' Paul said, 'but I got a recorded message saying your office was closed for a week and would reopen at nine this morning. So I told Clinton and he contacted Simon to ask when he could expect to receive the interest payment. The strange thing is, he told Clinton he hadn't borrowed any money and knew nothing of the mortgage. So, what's going on?'

It was at that moment Daniel knew Paul was onto him. He felt faint and his breakfast churned in his stomach. His mind was a blank; he could find no words to respond.

'During that conversation,' Paul went on, 'Simon told Clinton a valuer had contacted him some time ago to do a valuation of one of his properties, and he didn't know why.'

'Oh yes, that was a mistake,' Daniel said quickly. 'The valuer went to the wrong property. I promise you, your client will receive his interest by the end of the week.'

'That might be so, Daniel, but I've reported the matter to the Law Institute.'

Daniel's heart thudded in his chest. He knew his number was up and it was too late to try to convince Paul Ross of anything. He hung up.

Suddenly he felt spent. Despite the overseas holidays, the opulent lifestyle, the ease and comfort afforded by his wealth, the deception of the last few years had taken its toll. Closing his eyes, Daniel placed his arms on his desk and allowed his head to slump forward.

That night Daniel returned home from work at six o'clock. Putting his briefcase on the sideboard he walked straight onto the verandah. Despite the brisk winter air, his body was covered in a film of sweat and he felt breathless.

Lily followed him outside. 'What's wrong Daniel?' she asked. 'Why didn't you come and say hello?' Approaching him, she observed, 'You look pale; are you unwell?'

Daniel looked at her. 'I'm fine Lily; I just need some space. It's been a stressful day.'

She took his arm. 'Let's go for a walk. The exercise will do you good.'

'I'm too tired, Lily, and I want to be alone. I've got some things to think through. You go ahead . . .' Daniel was wiping the palms of his hands with a handkerchief and gazing up at the clouds.

'What are you looking at?' Lily asked.

'Those black storm clouds.'

'What about them?'

'They look threatening.'

As he lay in bed, Daniel picked over his conversation with Paul Ross. There was no way he could sleep. He got up and roamed the house like a man searching for something. He walked around the familiar rooms, but everything seemed suddenly strange: distorted and remote. He stopped at a window, paused for a moment and peered out at the street. He was there a long time.

Daniel left the house just as dawn was breaking across the city and arrived at work at seven o'clock. Walking into his office, he went straight to the liquor cabinet. He wiped his sweaty palms against his suit. Pouring himself a double scotch, he tossed it down his throat, forced open the window and threw himself out into the building's atrium, plummeting twenty-five floors to the tiles below.

Second Marriage

'This is a nice surprise,' I said as I opened the door and saw my mother standing on the porch. It was unlike her to drop in unannounced, and she looked ill at ease.

'How are you?' I said, concerned.

She gave a stiff smile and said, 'I'm well, Brendan.'

'Come in and let me make you a coffee.'

She followed me into the kitchen, where I switched on the kettle. 'So, to what do I owe the pleasure?' I asked.

A nervous smile played on her lips. After a momentary silence she said, 'There's something I want to tell you, Brendan.'

'Anything wrong?' I asked, immediately imagining the worst. Cancer?

She hesitated, her mouth quivering, then said, 'I've met somebody.'

I stared at her. A heavy silence shrouded the room. My father had died only a few months ago and I had no idea how to respond. Finally I stuttered, 'So . . . who is he?'

'His name is Alec Hatfield.'

'And where did you meet him?'

'I went out for dinner a few weeks ago with some friends and they introduced me to him. He's an acquaintance of theirs and was sitting at another table.'

As she spoke I felt my stomach churning.

'I'd like you to meet him, Brendan.'

I swallowed hard as my mother glanced anxiously up at me.

Sarah, my wife, walked into the room just then, breaking the awkward silence.

'Margaret, nice to see you. How are you?' she said.

'Good thanks, darling,' my mother said, giving her a tight smile.

'I'm sorry to disturb you, but Brendan and I have arrangements with friends for lunch; we're running late.'

'No problem, I don't want to hold you up,' my mother said. She sounded relieved.

'Let me walk you to the door,' I said, as I stood on shaky legs and turned off the kettle.

'I'll call to arrange a time for you and Sarah to come for dinner to meet Alec.'

'Okay,' I said as I opened the door.

That night I couldn't sleep. I got up, went down the hallway to the bathroom and splashed water on my face. I stood in front of the mirror, gripping the edge of the basin tightly.

I recalled Jake, a colleague, telling me about how his mother had married a man who turned out to be a parasite. When she became demented, her second husband began transferring two thousand dollars each week from her account to their joint account for living expenses. Several years later, the accountant had discovered that the man had moved a thousand dollars a week out of the joint account to his private account. According to the accountant, the second husband had stolen more than three hundred thousand dollars. When confronted by the woman's family, the second husband claimed he deserved the money and said, 'Where were you when your mother needed you?'

When I came into the kitchen the following morning, Sarah was sitting at the table in her dressing-gown, a glass of orange juice beside her plate of muesli.

'How did you sleep?' she asked.

'Badly, I was awake half the night,' I croaked.

'You do look a bit pale.'

'I feel shocking,' I said, heading for the espresso machine. 'Coffee?'

Sarah shook her head. 'What kept you up?'

'It's my mother,' I said with a sigh. 'I just can't get my head around the fact that she's in a new relationship so soon after my father's death.' I slammed the spent coffee into the compost bin.

'Yeah, I understand – it is pretty soon. But you know what? I'm pleased for her,' Sarah said.

'What?'

'I said, I'm pleased for her, Brendan. Your father always said she'd need another partner when he died, and I think he was probably right. Margaret hates being alone.'

'But Dad's been dead less than a year!' I concentrated on preparing my coffee.

Sarah was watching me intently. She came up behind me and placed her hands on my shoulders. In a soothing voice she said, 'Try to be happy for her, Brendan.'

I looked at Sarah blankly. My throat closed over and I swallowed hard. I waited for my coffee cup to fill then said, 'I'm going back to bed.'

Trembling, I lay on the bed with my eyes closed and thought about my father. I saw his face clearly – the soft brown eyes, high cheekbones, distinguished grey hair – the face I had lived with all my life. I could not imagine what it would be like to have someone take his place. I put my hands over my eyes. There was his face, or rather the way I felt about his face – his strong, melancholy spirit, his kindness and wisdom – still as clear as when he lived. I could feel a cold dread moving through me. Why I hadn't I seen this coming? Why hadn't I prepared myself?

There was a message for me on my voicemail when I got home the following Sunday morning from my walk. My mother had called a few minutes earlier and wanted me to call her back. I put away my runners and dialled her number. She picked up the phone after the first ring.

'Brendan, Alec and I are hosting a barbecue at my house tonight. Can you and Sarah join us?'

My heart sank; I wasn't ready for this. 'I don't know Mum . . .'

'What do you mean you don't know?' she said sharply.

'Um, it's just that I'm not sure whether Sarah's made arrangements for this evening.'

'Okay, I'll hold while you ask her,' she said firmly.

'Yes, just give me a minute.'

I put my hand over the phone and waited a moment, weighing up my options. I could refuse now, but sooner or later I would have to meet this man, so I was only putting off the inevitable.

'Yes, Mum, that'll be fine,' I said.

'Great!' she said brightly. 'We'll see you at six.'

'Uh-huh.'

'And Brendan, I think you'll like him.'

Before I could speak, she began to talk about Alec, his family, his career; it was far more than I wanted to know about this man usurping my father's place. Eventually she became aware of my silence and faltered. 'Well anyway, you'll see for yourself tonight.'

I hung up the phone and stood there a long time, staring down at it. Then I went to the kitchen, poured myself a glass of water and sat at the table. I wasn't thirsty but, lost in thought, I drank.

'Please try to be respectful,' Sarah said as we walked up the drive of my mother's house. 'I know this isn't easy for you.'

'Yes, of course I will,' I muttered as the blood pounded in my head. I pressed the doorbell with trembling fingers.

'G'day.' A barrel-chested man opened the door, his voice deep and gruff. He cleared his throat loudly and gave me a direct look. His eyes, clear and dark, locked onto mine and I felt a steely resolve. 'You must be Brendan,' he said.

'That's me,' I said, not quite meeting his eye.

Turning towards Sarah he bent forward, kissed her on the cheek and said, 'Pleased to meet you, Sarah.'

Then he inclined his head, indicating we should follow him down the hall. My mother was standing in the doorway of the dining room. Her hair was neatly brushed, she was wearing makeup, and it seemed her own private sun shone from her eyes. She looked at me and smiled.

There was a short, uncomfortable silence as we all stared at each other. I inhaled deeply and, grabbing at something to say, I remarked, 'Mum tells me you come from a large family, Alec.'

'Yes, I'm the youngest of eight,' he said. 'I was an accident – spoilt rotten. They all doted on me. Couldn't put a foot wrong.' He smirked.

'Let's sit down,' Mum said hastily, ushering us to our seats at the table.

I kept glancing at Alec throughout the meal. He talked over people, he imposed his opinions and he didn't listen to anyone else. Before we'd finished our first course he was enthusing about Tony Abbott and his contribution to Australia, his position on same-sex marriage and climate change. 'Everyone says the world is getting warmer, but we've just had the coldest summer on record – global warming's a farce!' he thundered.

Mum glanced at me anxiously, but I'd stopped listening. I found myself clutching my fork as if I were readying a weapon in my defence. Alec was a bombastic tyrant and I felt a violent fury towards him. What on earth was my mother doing with this vulgar man? He couldn't have been more different from my father, who was softly spoken, considerate and refined.

After we'd finished eating I waited for a break in the conversation. Alec was reassuring us that he'd always take good care of my mother, but as soon as he drew breath, I turned to Sarah and said, 'I have a busy day tomorrow. We should go.'

No doubt it was rude, but I'd had enough.

On the drive home, it started to rain heavily. Water banked up in gutters and overflowed onto the road.

'What do you make of Alec?' Sarah asked, raising her voice over the rhythmic swish of the windscreen wipers.

'I don't trust him,' I said.

'Really? Why not?'

'Remember when he said, "Your mother's a bit naïve, but I'll take care of her"?'

'Yes, I remember that. But why is that sinister?' Sarah asked.

'Well, I know it sounds ridiculous, but at that moment I thought to myself: there will be trouble from this relationship.'

'But why, Brendan? Aren't you being a bit alarmist?'

'Maybe,' I conceded, 'but I can't help suspecting that he's self-serving and crafty. That patronising speech about my mother confirmed my gut feeling that he's out to take advantage of her vulnerability.'

Sarah sighed loudly. 'Oh Brendan, I think Jake's story about his mother's disastrous second marriage is clouding your thinking. Be careful not to make assumptions about Alec. Do you really think he's that sort of person?'

'I don't know, perhaps not. But when you make hasty decisions on the rebound, such as my mother has just done, there can only be trouble.'

'You're being a bit of a prophet of doom, I have to say. But look, if you've got such deep concerns about Alec – which clearly you do – why don't you talk to your mother about your misgivings?' Sarah said.

'I'm not sure I feel comfortable doing that,' I said, peering through the rain-drenched windscreen.

'Why? You and your mother have a good relationship. It's always seemed very frank and open to me.'

'We do. But if she asks me to justify my concerns, what am I going to tell her? That I have a gut feeling? Seems a bit weak, don't you think?'

'I guess,' Sarah said. Then she added, 'Let's give this some time and allow the situation to declare itself. It's early days,' she said, placing a hand on my forearm.

Awake again that night, I got out of bed and looked out the window at the deserted street illuminated by a pale moon. I became aware that I was grinding my teeth as I ruminated on Alec's intentions. Was he after my mother's money or did he genuinely love her? Irrespective of his motives, I didn't think I had the right to shape my mother's life and I decided not to burden her with my concerns.

About a month later, Sarah and I met my mother and Alec for dinner. Alec sat opposite me and Mum was seated beside me and across from Sarah. I saw Mum's eyes flicker in my direction as she and Sarah chatted. I felt her hand on my arm, her fingers tightening momentarily.

'Alec and I are moving in together,' she said suddenly. Her voice became husky, so she cleared her throat and continued, 'He's moving in to my house.'

Alec looked at me and I detected a challenge in his gaze. He was silent a moment, nodding his head. Then he said, 'We want to be together.'

I stared into his bear-like face, then looked at Sarah. My heart began to pound. I turned towards my mother and, selecting my words carefully, said, 'Don't you think it's a bit too soon, Mum? Dad hasn't been dead a year and you were married for almost fifty—'

'Yes, it has happened quickly, but Alec has been given notice on his rental unit so I suggested he move in with me.'

'Brendan, your mother isn't getting any younger,' Alec interrupted. 'Don't you think it would be good if I took care of her?'

I gaped at him.

'So when are you proposing to move in, Alec?' Sarah asked.

'At the end of the month.'

His words rang in my ears. Suddenly I felt nauseated and lightheaded.

'Alec's right,' my mother said. 'I don't feel safe living by myself. To tell you the truth, I'm becoming forgetful. And it's comforting to have Alec with me all the time. The way I see it, it's fortuitous that he's been given notice on his unit. I really want him to move in with me.'

Alec cleared his throat, looked at me and said, 'You need to be aware of one of my conditions for moving in. I've told Margaret I'll only move in if I can stay in the house for the rest of my life, and if she dies before me, her estate pays the outgoings on the property.'

I felt faint. I couldn't believe the audacity of the man. 'That house was purchased with my mother's inheritance!' I snapped.

Alec straightened his spine and folded his arms in a gesture of defiance.

'What happens if Mum gets knocked over by a bus and you find another partner? Do you expect to live in that house courtesy of my mother?' I said, my voice rising.

'So, what's wrong with that?' Alec said. Then he pushed back his chair, turned to my mother and said, 'Let's go, Margaret.'

My mother looked at Sarah, eyes wide with panic. She hated confrontation and I was once again stunned that she'd chosen such a belligerent man. She remained rooted to her seat while Alec stormed out of the restaurant.

I felt a mountainous rage, but I followed him out the front door and stood awkwardly under the restaurant awning as the wind lashed the bare winter trees and Alec glared out into the night.

Before I could speak he leant towards me and said, 'We love each other, Brendan. We want to be together.'

'I get that Alec. But why do you insist on living in my mother's house indefinitely?'

'Look, I'm seventy-five years old. It's not easy for me to move house; I want this to be my last stop.'

'And why should her estate pay your outgoings?' I said.

Suddenly, a flash of lightning cut across the sky and thunder exploded overhead. Alec jumped and his face was momentarily lit up and then fell into darkness again.

'Because I won't be able to afford it on my pension, of course.'

I feared I was about to lose my mother but I also felt powerless to interfere in her decisions. 'Let's go back inside,' I said. My knees felt unsteady and my mouth was dry.

Once we were back at the table Alec turned to me and said, 'So, do we have your approval, Brendan?'

'Alec, you don't need my approval. You're adults and I don't have any power to stop you.'

'You're right, Brendan: we don't need your approval. But it would sit easier with me if I had your blessing,' Mum said.

I started to respond. I felt the words deep in my throat but I could not get them out. I swallowed and took a deep breath. 'Well, I'm not sure I can give you that right now, Mum.'

I decided to give my mother a wide berth. The sudden changes in her life were too much to deal with, so although I called her periodically, I avoided meeting her. When she rang to invite us over, I made the usual excuses of work and family commitments.

About six weeks after Alec moved in, I received a phone call from Mum's sister, asking me if I was concerned about my mother's health. Aunty Joan had visited Mum recently and said she seemed confused at times, and her memory was failing.

'Aunty Joan, I haven't seen my mother for some time,' I confessed. 'I'm really struggling to get my head around her new relationship . . .'

'Well, I suggest you put your own issues aside, Brendan,' she said tartly. 'Your mother needs you.'

Disconcerted, I mentioned the phone call to Sarah.

'Joan's right,' she said. It's about time you paid your mother a visit.'

'But I can't stand the sight of that man!' I protested.

'Brendan, your mother isn't getting any younger and if something were to happen to her, you don't want to be left with all that regret and guilt about your estrangement. It's time you looked beyond your own feelings.'

I knew Sarah was right so the next morning I called my mother to arrange a visit.

𝓅

A few days later I was seated in the lounge at my mother's house. She and Alec sat on the sofa opposite, Alec buried in the *Australian*.

'It's time they got those refugees off Manus Island and sent them back where they came from,' he remarked.

I ignored him and turned to my mother. 'How are you?' I said, looking directly into her eyes.

'I'm all right,' she said in a small voice.

'Are you sure? How's your memory?'

'I'm feeling fine. Why the questions? Why are you interrogating me?'

Alec put down his newspaper and watched her attentively.

'I spoke with Aunty Joan the other day; she's worried about you,' I said.

'Jane doesn't know what she's talking about,' Mum huffed.

'Joan,' I said.

Alec caught my eye and shook his head.

'She doesn't know what she's talking about,' Mum said again.

Alec looked at my mother with concern, his face softening. 'Are you okay, darling?' He gently placed a hand against her face.

'When was the last time you visited your GP?' I said.

'I can't remember,' Mum said, her voice flat and dull.

'Well, maybe it's time for a check-up.'

Alec looked at Mum and said, 'I'm happy to take you. We'll go together.' He gazed into my mother's eyes and I couldn't help but notice the loving look that passed between them. 'Brendan's right,' Alec added. 'We should get you checked out.'

As I drove home, it occurred to me that Alec must have been aware of my mother's developing confusion. I wondered why he hadn't mentioned it. Was it because he loved her and couldn't face the possibility of her being sick? Or worse still – of losing her?

One Thursday afternoon, I was reading when the phone rang. Outside it was a cold, dismal day and raindrops spattered the windows.

'Brendan, it's Alec.'

'How are you?' I replied coolly.

I waited for him to continue but he allowed the silence to grow. Then he said, 'I need to tell you, your mother's not well.'

I took a deep breath. 'What's wrong?'

'Margaret and I have just come from Dr Walsh's surgery . . .'

'Who is Dr Walsh?'

'He's the specialist your mother's GP sent us to see.'

'Back up a minute,' I said quickly. 'What don't I know about this?'

'You do know I took Margaret to see her GP, Dr Sullivan.'

'Yes, and . . . '

'He asked her a lot of questions about the family . . .'

'Such as?' I interrupted him.

'He asked whether Margaret had any children or grandchildren.'

'And how did Mum reply?'

'Frankly, she was confused. She said she didn't have any children and would have to check up about whether she had any grandchildren.'

I felt my stomach drop. How could she have declined so rapidly?

'Then he asked her questions about her assets,' Alec continued.

'For example?' I croaked.

'She said she owned a house in Toorak, but she had no idea about its value and when he asked whether she had any other assets she didn't seem to understand the question.'

I watched the rain running down the window. I felt like crying.

'The bottom line is, Dr Sullivan said your mother is cognitively impaired and recommended she see a specialist,' Alec said.

I took a deep breath to calm my racing heart.

'So Dr Sullivan sent Margaret off for a series of tests,' Alec continued, 'and the results went straight to Dr Walsh. We've just come from his surgery.' He paused, then said with a heavy sigh, 'Brendan, I'm sorry to tell you, but your mother has Alzheimer's.'

My knees felt suddenly weak and I was momentarily lost for words. Finally I managed to say, 'How is she?'

'Fragile, I think is the best way to describe her,' Alec said, his voice betraying the emotion he too was feeling at this sudden twist of fate.

'Can I have a quick word with her?'

'She's asleep. It's been an overwhelming day.'

'Don't wake her,' I said. 'Can Sarah and I drop in this evening?'

'Of course,' Alec said. 'I'm sure Margaret would love to see you.'

'Thanks for coming,' Alec said as he opened the door. We followed him down the hall into the lounge. Mum was perched on the sofa, looking pale and worn. As we entered, she started to rise.

'Don't get up, Margaret,' Sarah said.

'I'm all right,' my mother said in a thin voice.

'Mum, it's good to see you,' I said, sitting beside her on the sofa and placing my arm around her frail shoulders. 'How are you doing?'

She didn't respond. Instead, she looked at Alec, seeming to seek his reassurance and guidance. Alec smiled at her warmly and a silence fell as I became aware of their intimacy and the obvious trust between them.

Finally, Alec said, 'It's all right, Margaret. Nobody's going to make you do anything you don't want to.' He took her hand in his bear-like paw and her whole body seemed to slacken with relief. 'I'll look after you. I won't let you go into a nursing home.'

I felt a lump form in my throat. 'That's very kind of you Alec,' I said, choked with emotion.

'I wouldn't want it any other way,' Alec said. Giving me a direct look, he said, 'Brendan, I love your mother. I'll take good care of her.'

I felt overwhelmed by his loyalty, and also queasy about my hasty judgement of him. Sensing my inability to respond, Sarah turned to Mum and said, 'It seems you are in very good hands, Margaret.'

Bradley Engineering

Vicki had spent the day trudging around the city looking for work. She'd walked from one café to the next, answering question after question, and when each manager asked her what she'd been doing the past eight years, and why she, an experienced accountant, was seeking work as a waitress, she lied, knowing that the truth would kill off any job opportunities.

By late afternoon, exhausted and worried about how she would continue to pay her rent, she dragged herself up the stairs to her flat. Her teenage son, Oscar, still in his school uniform, was washing dishes at the sink. They exchanged a wary greeting and Vicki slumped at the scarred table under the window that looked out onto the fire escape.

To Oscar, everything about his mother was now strange; he felt like he no longer knew who she was. Her short chestnut hair and round face looked the same, sort of, but she had more lines and her hair was greying at the roots.

'I'm exhausted,' Vicki sighed, and shrugged out of her coat.

'Any luck?' Oscar asked tentatively.

He poured her a glass of water, placed it on the table and sat down opposite her. He could feel his mother scanning the landscape of his face, taking in every detail. He was only fourteen years old but he already had fine facial hair and his eyebrows were thickening.

'You're so grown up,' Vicki said, a hint of wistfulness in her voice.

'That's what happens in eight years, Mum.'

Ignoring his curt response Vicki said, 'To get back to your question, Oscar: no, no luck. It's impossible to find work.'

'Something will come up sooner or later, Mum.'

'I'm not so sure. It's not easy for someone with my background ...' She sighed and fiddled with the glass.

'Can't you even get work as a waitress?'

Vicki paused for a moment, fidgeted uncomfortably in her chair and looked past Oscar at the clean dishes stacked neatly on the dish rack. 'Oscar, I've been home for two weeks and we haven't really had a proper conversation. You haven't even told me what it was like, living with Uncle Robert, out on the farm ...'

'Eight years is a long time,' he said flatly.

'C'mon, it wasn't that bad I hope?' Vicki said, a pleading look in her eyes.

'Robert lives a long way out. I felt really isolated and I missed my friends,' Oscar said, looking away from his mother.

'Yes, I'm sure it wasn't easy ...'

Oscar started to get to his feet, but changed his mind and sat back down again. He looked across the table at Vicki, his face tight.

Vicki sighed. 'It was generous of Robert to take you in. Had it not been for him I don't know who would have cared for you.'

Oscar seemed about to say something, but he faltered and stopped.

'Say it. What's bothering you?' Vicki coaxed.

The boy hesitated. He felt so many competing emotions towards his mother: anger at her recklessness, resentment at her selfishness – and yet he still loved her.

Noticing his anguish, Vicki felt a lump form in her throat. 'I hope we can get to know each other again, Oscar. Those prison visits were so difficult and strained.'

'To be honest, Mum, I don't feel like I know you at all.'

There was a heavy silence as Oscar stared out the window and Vicki picked at the chipped polish on her fingernails.

Finally, Oscar gave his mother a straight look and said, 'Why did you do it?'

Vicki felt the blood drain from her face. She turned and stared blankly at the fire escape. The silence lasted for a long moment, then she faced Oscar and tried to find the words to answer him.

'Did it cross your mind that your actions would have an effect on me?' he asked in a voice thick with anger.

'You know the old cliché,' Vicki said, 'criminals never think they're going to get caught. So, to be honest, no. I didn't give any thought to how my crime might affect you. If anything, I was sure I'd make us a lot of money – set us up for life.'

Oscar's face contorted with disgust. 'But how could you think that stealing from your boss was okay? And why would you think I'd be fine about living off dirty money?' he said, his voice rising.

'Oscar, please, calm down,' Vicki said. 'I didn't think you would ever find out where I got the money from. I just wanted to make our life easier . . .'

'Really? But don't you have any morals? Any conscience?'

Vicki shrugged. 'Funny you should ask that. I've given a lot of thought to that question. There's plenty of time to think in prison.' She paused. 'Look, maybe I don't.' She glanced up at him. 'But I'm glad you do.'

In the silence, Vicki reflected on where Oscar might have learnt his values. She thought about her brother, Robert. He had always been a decent man with an unequivocal sense of right and wrong.

'I guess you must have learnt it from your uncle. Another thing to be grateful to him for . . . '

Oscar stood up. 'This conversation is too much, Mum,' Oscar said. 'I'm going to my room.'

Vicki lay awake and listened to the sound of a distant siren. As she reflected on her conversation with Oscar, she could feel a metallic coldness moving through her. In jail, she had pondered why she had stolen from her employer. What had led her to do it? She thought about how values are transmitted from parents to children. By a twist of fate, it seemed Oscar had learnt something from Robert; but where had she learnt her values?

Staring at the cracks in the ceiling, she suddenly remembered a heated argument between her parents when she was about seventeen years old. She had been in the kitchen doing her maths homework while her parents were in the living room. Her mother was saying that Alan Bond was a real bastard, that he had defrauded the Bond Corporation of billions of dollars.

Defending him, her father had said that Bond was a great Australian, he'd won the America's Cup for his country and accumulated enough wealth to make people jealous. Vicki realised now that it was as if his affluence and status justified the means by which he'd attained them. 'Every businessman is a little bit crooked,' his father had said. 'Don't be so naïve.'

Vicki tossed off her blanket and got up to close the window. As she lay back down, she remembered thinking at the time that her father was right, that the ends *do* justify the means. She had dismissed her mother as a self-righteous fool.

Now she wondered to what extent her father's values had influenced her. Clearly she had absorbed the message that obtaining money by any means was acceptable, even if it meant harming others. But could she blame her father for her actions after all these years?

P

Oscar's alarm shrieked at seven o'clock and he struggled to rouse himself. It seemed as if he'd only just fallen into a deep sleep. As usual, he'd been woken by a nightmare. Last night he'd dreamt that the police were banging on the front door, coming to arrest his mother. He'd woken in an icy sweat.

Eventually, he dragged himself down the hall to the bathroom, splashed water on his face and stumbled into the kitchen.

Vicki placed a glass of orange juice on the table and said, 'You look terrible, Oscar. Didn't you get any sleep?'

'I had nightmares,' Oscar said. He took a deep breath and continued. 'I woke with a fright and started to think about our conversation last night, then I couldn't get back to sleep.'

Vicki nodded. 'I hardly slept either. I remembered an incident in my childhood that obviously had a deep effect on me. My father worshipped businessmen like Alan Bond and Laurie Connell – you won't have heard of them, but they walked a very fine line between the straight and the crooked, and both of them fell off more than once. To Dad, though, their wealth made them heroes, and it didn't matter how they made it.' Vicki stepped back and leaned against the sink. 'My father taught me some bad lessons,' she said.

Oscar grunted, pushed back his chair and grabbed a carton of milk from the fridge. As he sat down he turned to his mother, ignoring what she'd just said. 'When did you decide to steal the money?'

Vicki was silent for a moment then, swallowing her shame, she said, 'My boss, Steve, had invited all the staff to morning tea to celebrate my ten years of service at Bradley Engineering. I was their finance manager by then.'

Oscar looked at his mother expectantly. He'd never heard the whole story, or anything much at all from his mother.

Vicki went on. 'During the morning tea, Steve told me that he was going on holidays and that, in his absence, I'd be sole signatory on the bank accounts. He said he trusted me, that I had proved myself through all my years of service to the company.'

Vicki fell silent. She exhaled a deep sigh. 'That's when it started.'

Oscar shook his head in disbelief.

Vicki continued. 'All I could see was the opportunity to do what I'd always wanted – to have enough money to invest in the stock market. The timing was perfect, the stock market had collapsed and if I invested wisely I knew I could make a lot of money.'

Oscar sat frozen, silent. Part of him didn't want to hear any more, but the other part wanted to know the full story, at last.

'So I decided I would prepare dummy invoices from creditors, pay money into my own account and use it to trade shares.'

'But weren't you afraid you'd get caught?' Oscar interjected.

'As I said last night, I didn't give any thought to consequences, Oscar. I was captivated by the opportunity. I thought I had to take advantage of the situation and make as much money as I could.'

'But didn't you feel bad about Steve? He trusted you,' Oscar said, shifting in his seat.

'I wasn't worried about Steve,' Vicki said with a dismissive wave of her hand. 'His father is a very wealthy man and everything had always come easily for him. He'd inherited his father's business and had never had to struggle for anything. In my twisted logic I felt a bit like Robin Hood. I was sharing the wealth around.' She gave him a wry smile.

Oscar stood abruptly, his chair scraping against the tiled floor. 'That's bullshit Mum and you know it,' he said as he marched out of the room.

To break the tension, that afternoon Vicki insisted they walk down the street to Tom and Tilly's Ice Cream Parlour. She hoped the outing would divert Oscar's attention from her crime, that they might even find some common ground – something good to bridge the chasm between them.

But as soon as they sat down at the laminated table, Oscar leaned forward in his chair and fixed his mother with a stern expression. 'When you stole from your boss, it *was* the first time you'd done it, wasn't it? Or had you stolen money before?' he demanded.

Vicki shifted uneasily in her seat. She glanced out the window, unable to hold Oscar's gaze. His words ricocheted around her head and triggered another memory. She wanted to be honest, but how could she regain her son's respect if she revealed yet another dark side of her character?

She took a deep breath, stared straight ahead and said, 'Sort of.'

'What does that mean?' Oscar spat. 'Yes or no?'

'As a student I worked as a waitress in a coffee shop . . .' Vicki's skin felt clammy and the room seemed drained of air. Reluctantly, she went on. 'Sometimes, when customers paid their bill, I'd pocket a few dollars and put the rest in the cash register.'

Oscar blinked at his mother in disbelief. 'And you didn't get caught?'

'No, I didn't. But I used the money to buy books for uni—'

'And you think that makes it okay?' Oscar said, his voice tight with anger. He stood up and tossed his ice cream into the bin. 'I've heard enough of your justifications,' he growled, and stormed out.

P

The tension between them persisted into dinner. After a long silence, in which Oscar refused to raise his eyes from the table, he slowly lifted his head and said, 'So, tell me, Mum. How did Steve discover the fraud? How did you get caught?'

'Didn't Robert explain any of this to you?' Vicki asked, growing more and more despairing with his endless questions.

'No, he didn't. He refused to discuss it. Besides, I want to hear it from you.'

Vicki gave an involuntary shiver. Talking about her fraud had brought back all her years at Bradley Engineering. She knew that her son had a right to know everything about what she had done, but she hated feeling so vulnerable, so exposed. 'This isn't easy for me, Oscar; it is very painful to revisit those years. But I owe you the unvarnished truth, so here goes.' She took a deep breath, then continued. 'A few months after that morning tea, Steve came into my office and told me that Bradley Engineering was tight on liquidity and he had no choice but to put the business into administration.'

Oscar looked at her, perplexed, his soup spoon halfway to his mouth. 'What does that mean?'

'It means that the business was in trouble and Steve had appointed an expert to sort out the financial difficulties.'

'Okay, I understand. Go on.'

'Within days the administrator appointed an auditor to comb through the books and Steve asked me to assist him,' Vicki said. 'I still remember the name: Baer Accountants and Auditors. Brendan was kind . . .'

Oscar put down his spoon. 'So, you must have been terrified.'

'Yes, at that moment I knew my number was up,' Vicki said, pushing her soup bowl aside. Her head had begun to pound. After a pause, she continued, her voice trembling. 'Two months into the audit, Steve marched into my office and closed the door behind him. He said there were twenty million dollars missing from the bank and demanded an explanation.'

Oscar swallowed the lump in his throat. 'So what did you say? How did you react?'

'To be honest, I can't remember very much, my mind went blank. But I do remember feeling like I wanted to vomit.'

Oscar stared at his mother, whose face had turned deathly pale. There was a long moment of silence. Finally Vicki said, 'When Steve told me I was his most trusted employee, that I needed to help him sort out the mess, I finally broke down and confessed. He looked me in the eye and said sadly, "I never thought you would lie to me."'

Oscar saw a flicker of pain in Vicki's eyes. 'And then what happened?' he asked.

'He walked over to my desk, picked up the phone and called the police. When he left the room he turned and gave me such a look . . .'

Vicki stood up and took a bottle of vodka from the cabinet. She poured herself a shot and returned to the table.

'Mum, can I ask you one more question?' Oscar said.

'Why not?' she said bitterly.

'One time when Uncle Robert and I visited you in jail, I heard you say that you thought your sentence was unfair. And I never understood why.'

'It's true. I did say that, and I still believe it.' There was a glint of defiance in Vicki's eyes as she continued. 'Look, Oscar, I know

I made a mistake. But those shares were sold for twenty-five million dollars and all that money went straight to the administrator.'

'So you think you should have received a more lenient sentence because of that?' Oscar asked.

Vicki took another swig of vodka. 'I know they had to send a strong message about what I did, but I made the company five million dollars,' she said, slamming the glass on the table.

Oscar leaned away from his mother. 'But didn't Bradley Engineering go broke because of you?' he said.

'No, that's not true, Oscar. According to the judge, my actions only *contributed* to the company's insolvency,' Vicki said, her voice rising with each word.

Oscar looked at his mother sceptically. 'You're still trying to wriggle out of this, aren't you? And clearly you still believe that money trumps everything.' He shook his head in weary disbelief.

Vicki fell silent. 'You may be right, Oscar, I don't know,' she said. 'But there's one thing I do know: I love you more than anything in the world and I will do anything to mend the rift between us.'

Oscar sighed heavily. 'You need to give me some time.' He paused. 'I still can't get my head around it.'

'I know, Oscar. And I guess that's my real punishment. I just hope it's not a life sentence.'

*

Acknowledgements

I was privileged to have the assistance of many people while writing these stories, which would not have been possible without the help of Nadine Davidoff. I learned a remarkable amount about writing from her. She has been a source of great insight and guidance and I owe her a huge debt of gratitude for her incredibly generous support. I am truly grateful to her. She gave willingly of her time and I have benefited from her understanding, acumen and direction.

I am grateful for the help of Nan McNab. Her extensive work in editing these stories has been instrumental in making them infinitely better. I have greatly benefited from her insights, counsel and assistance. She has been remarkably patient with me, nothing was too difficult, and she was a pleasure to work with.

My heartfelt thanks to Bob Sessions for his support and guidance in the publication process. I have also benefited from the endless hours of typing and retyping by Noni Carr-Howard. Sam and Diana Seoud set aside a table at their café, Dundas and Faussett, to enable me to write.

Finally, many friends have been there for me along this journey. They are too numerous to name – you know who you are. Thank you for your support and encouragement. And last but not least, thank you to my family for your enthusiastic support and helping me keep everything in perspective.

Bernard Marin AM was born in 1950 and graduated from the Prahran College of Advanced Education in Melbourne in 1970. He established his accounting practice in 1981 and currently works with the staff and partners of the practice as a consultant. Bernard has held a number of positions on various boards, including: Treasurer – Melbourne Writers Festival (2005–16), Koorie Heritage Trust (2000–08), and Liberty Victoria (de facto, 1984–92); board member – Australian Centre for Jewish Civilisation (2009–15), Reichstein Foundation (2011–12), Melbourne Community Foundation (2009–10), and Koorie Heritage Trust (2000–12).

Bernard is the author of *Selection in Human Resource Accounting* (1982); a memoir, *My Father, My Father* (Scribe, 2002); *Good as Gold: A Novel* (Harvard Publications, 2017); and *Stories of Remembering and Forgetting* (Harvard Publications, 2019). Bernard lives in Melbourne with his wife, Wendy.